# The Interview

Phil M. Williams

# A Note from Phil

Dear Reader,

If you're interested in receiving my novel *Against the Grain* for free and/or reading many of my other titles for free or discounted, go to the following link: http://www.PhilWBooks.com.

You're probably thinking, *What's the catch?* There is no catch.

Sincerely,
Phil M. Williams

# Chapter 1: Mo and Pickin' Ain't Easy

Mo was in bed, flicking his thumb on his cell phone, scrolling his Instagram feed. He paused on an advertisement for Total Sports Agency. He'd seen the ad at least ten times over the past week. In the image, Antonio Brown, the former Steeler great, shook hands with his agent. The caption read *This could be you. We're looking for former Division 1 athletes who can relate to our clients. Now hiring for paid internships. Click here to apply.*

Mo imagined being the sports agent in the picture. He sighed. *Yeah, right.*

A direct message appeared on his Instagram. Mo clicked on the DM.

> **Glen**: Hey, Mo. I know it's been forever, but I heard you were back home, and I wanted to see how you're doing.

Mo hadn't talked to Glen since their freshman year in high school, five years ago, but Mo didn't feel much like reminiscing. He had nearly reached out last year—when Glen's parents had died in a fiery Tesla accident—but Mo hadn't been sure how his message would be received. Mo closed his direct messages, not responding.

"*Shit.*" Mo sucked air through his teeth, realizing that Glen would see that his message had been read without a response. Mo should've left it unread. Glen had always been oversensitive to real and imagined slights.

Mo shrugged. "Fuck it."

He went back to the advertisement and clicked the link, taking Mo to TotalSportsAgency.com/internship. Again, he saw the image of Antonio Brown shaking hands with the agent. Mo scrolled down, reading more about the internship. Benefits included competitive pay, health care, college tuition reimbursement, and law school reimbursement.

The page invited him to *Join the Team! Please click here to download the employment portal.*

Mo clicked the link. A message appeared on his phone, asking him whether to give TotalSportsAgency.com access to his phone.

He hovered his finger over his phone, his stomach turning with discomfort. *This must be a scam.*

The side door slammed downstairs. Mo set his phone on his bedside table and sat up in bed, his bare feet on the floor. Heavy boots stomped up the stairs, followed by a hard knock at Mo's bedroom door.

Mo ran his hands over his tight curls, from back to front. "Yeah?"

Mo's father entered the room, wearing his coveralls, and bringing a garbage smell with him. His name, Reggie, was stitched over his right pectoral. Horizons Waste Management was stitched over his left pectoral.

Reggie approached the bedside, scanning Mo's room along the way, and scowling at the clothes on the floor and the dirty dishes on the desk. "You just gettin' up?"

Mo cleared his throat. "No. I've been looking for a job."

Reggie crossed his arms over his chest. "In your pajamas?"

Mo frowned at his father and grabbed his phone from his bedside table. He tapped Yes on the screen, giving TotalSportsAgency.com access to his phone, and starting the download. Then, he showed the screen to his father. "Applications are all online now. I'm just waiting for this employment portal to download."

Reggie dropped his arms and squinted at the screen. "What kinda job is it?"

"It's an internship to become a sports agent."

"Internship? Does it pay?"

"Yeah. It pays."

"When do you find out if you got the job?"

Mo let out a breath. "I just downloaded the portal. I still have to fill out the application."

Reggie shook his head. "You need a job now, son."

Mo stood from his bed, standing a few inches taller than his father. "That's what I'm doing. Get off my back."

Reggie raised one side of his mouth in contempt. "Oh, you think you can talk to me like you're grown?"

"I'm doing the best I can."

Reggie cocked his head. "You think you're doin' the best you can? I could get you a job tomorrow—"

"As what? A picker?"

"They're desperate for pickers. Pays $20 an hour."

Mo grabbed his jeans from the floor. "I'm not picking up garbage." Mo folded his jeans and set them on the bed, suddenly embarrassed by the condition of his room.

"I was only a picker for four years until I got my route. You could get a route in two years."

Mo shook his head. "No. That's your life. It won't be mine."

Reggie's wiry muscles tensed under his coveralls. "It's an honest livin'. Ain't no shame in it. Paid for this house and everything in it."

"It's just not for me. Mom never wanted me to do a manual labor job. What if I get hurt?"

"Your mom didn't want you playin' football neither."

Mo winced. "I should've listened."

"Football didn't get your ass kicked out of school."

Mo sat on the edge of his bed. "I know, Dad. I don't wanna talk about it."

"You had your chance to get an education." Reggie pointed a craggy finger at Mo. "You pissed it away."

Mo held out his hands. "You think I don't know that? I think about it every single day."

"It's time to grow up, son. What's done is done."

Mo swallowed the lump in his throat.

"You can't be here doin' nothin'. You got one month. You don't get a job by then, you're out. You're on your own." Reggie arched his eyebrows. "Got me?"

"Yeah. I got you."

Reggie left the room.

Mo thought about his mother. She had died of brain cancer fourteen months ago. Fourteen months and five days to be exact. Mo thought about the time he'd broken his wrist when he had wrecked his bicycle. His mother had been opposed to buying him a bike, but Mo had begged and begged, and she'd relented. In the hospital, while Mo and his mother had waited for the doctor to examine his wrist, she'd said, "My biggest fear is that I'll outlive you. I don't think I can live without you. You have to promise me that you'll be careful."

*She'd be so disappointed with what I've done.* Mo hung his head.

# Chapter 2: Cora and The Roasted Bean

Toast popped from the toaster. Cora grabbed the bread gingerly, dropping the hot toast onto two plates. The expiration date on the mayonnaise read 5-3-2021. It was a week old, but it wasn't the first time she'd eaten expired food, much more than a week past the date too. Cora made bologna and cheese sandwiches, with a side of potato chips.

She took one plate to the living room on a tray with a can of soda. The television blared. The curtains were drawn. Cora's paintings adorned the walls, none of the landscapes with a proper frame. Cora's mother, Stella, watched a trashy talk show, slouched on the couch, her feet propped on an ottoman that didn't match. Cora placed the tray on Stella's mushy midsection.

Stella grunted and grabbed the tray, never taking her eyes off the television.

Cora went back to the kitchen and sat at the table with her lunch. She scrolled on her Instagram feed, as she ate her sandwich. She stopped on a picture of Allie Gillespie in a boutique clothing store, posing with Taylor Oliver.

The caption read *Besties for life!*

*That's what she used to say about us.* Cora wondered why Allie never blocked her on Instagram. *She does have 14,000 followers. Maybe she didn't notice.* Cora bit her lower lip. *Not likely. She probably wants me to see how happy she is without me.* Cora sighed. *I need to get a life.*

She scrolled down her feed, pausing on an advertisement she'd seen at least a dozen times in the past few days. It was a picture of a young woman designing a logo on a laptop, with an older woman standing next to her, pointing at the screen, both smiling.

The caption read *Total Graphic Design. Paid internships available for aspiring graphic designers. Click here to join the team!*

Cora clicked on the link, taking her to TotalGraphicDesign.com/internship. Here, she learned a little more about the internship. It paid $25 per hour, offered health insurance and tuition reimbursement. It only required a high school diploma and an original portfolio displaying her creativity. She had her diploma and plenty of drawings and paintings. She clicked the employment portal. A message appeared, asking her if she wanted to give TotalGraphicDesign.com access to her phone.

*This is sus.*

Cora checked the time on her phone. *Shit. I'm going to be late.* She tapped No to the permission. Then she took her dishes to the sink, leaving them unwashed, knowing they'd still be there when she returned from work. She left the house with her purse over her shoulder, saying goodbye to her mother, and receiving a grunt in return.

Outside, the sun shone bright, with a pleasant breeze. The mailman walked up the cracked concrete walkway. He smiled at Cora and handed her the mail. "Here you go."

"Thank you," Cora replied, taking the mail. She turned to the mailbox next to the front door, with the intention of dropping the mail inside, but the letter on top caught her attention. It was from Villanova Collections Agency. Cora flipped through the mail. Two letters had Past Due written on the outside of the envelope. One was from Keystone Mortgage Lenders. Cora's heart pounded. The bologna turned in her stomach. She opened the envelope from Keystone and scanned the statement. Her mother was sixty days past due on the mortgage. They owed two months, plus late fees and interest.

Cora took the mail inside and slammed the door behind her.

Stella glared at her. "*Hey.*"

Cora stalked to her mother and snatched the remote from the armrest. She hit the Power button, silencing the television.

"What the hell?" Stella asked.

Cora slapped the stack of mail on the coffee table. "You told me the bills were paid."

Stella groaned as she sat upright, placing her stocking feet on the floor. "They are."

"Really?" Cora picked up the stack of mail. She dealt them like cards. "Here's a past due bill. Here's another. Here's another."

Stella glanced at the letters. "Those are bullshit. We don't have to pay those."

Cora slapped the letter from Keystone Mortgage Lenders on the coffee table. "What about the house? Do we have to pay this bill?"

Stella grabbed the open envelope and scowled at Cora. "This isn't for you."

"I gave you all my money! You said it was paid."

Stella pointed the envelope at Cora. "This is none of your business. I'm handling it."

Cora clenched her fists, her face beet red. "You're a liar."

Stella stared at her daughter for a long beat with narrowed eyes. "I wish it would've been *you.*"

Cora drew back, stunned. Her face contorted and reddened. "So do I." She left the house, slamming the door in her wake. She fast-walked to work, nearly three miles, wiping tears as she went.

The tears had dried by the time she made it to the Shoppes at Devonshire, but her face was a blotchy mess. She walked through the outdoor shopping center, passing clothing, shoe, and jewelry stores. She entered The Roasted Bean. A Now Hiring sign hung in the window.

Five people waited in line. Martina waited on a slight man, who read the menu on the wall behind the counter. Martina wore the khaki pants and a green Roasted Bean polo like Cora, but Martina had blue hair, earrings running up her earlobes like rivets, and a nose ring. She wore a Black Lives Matter bracelet and a pin that read *Make ME a sandwich.* Cora usually waited on the customers, while Martina made the coffee.

Martina flashed Cora the evil eye as she approached the counter.

Cora mouthed, *Sorry,* as she walked around the counter and took Martina's place behind the register and in front of the slight man. "Welcome to The Roasted Bean. What can I get for you?" Cora asked, with a saccharine smile, as she placed her purse under the counter.

The man still read the menu through thick glasses. "Um, ... uh, ... I'm ... not sure. Uh, ... what's a macchiato?" He pronounced it *machado.*

*I'm pretty sure that's someone's last name.* "A macchiato is an espresso with a little frothy milk."

"*Hmm.* I don't really like milk. I'm lactose intolerant. Um, ... uh, ... let me think. You have a lot of choices. I usually get coffee at McDonalds, but I thought I'd treat myself today. My neighbor told me this is the best place for coffee."

"That's nice of your neighbor to say," Cora replied.

The slight man smacked his lips several times. His teeth were yellow. "What's an espresso?"

A few groans came from the customers in line.

The greasy man in the back of the line said, "Maybe you should open another register."

Martina rolled her eyes, hiding behind the machines.

"It's a strong black coffee made by forcing steam through ground coffee beans," Cora said.

"*Hmm.* Um, ... I'm not sure," the slight man said. "I don't really like strong coffee. It tastes too much like coffee. I mean, I like coffee, just not too much. You know?"

"Sure. I understand."

The woman behind the slight man answered her cell phone.

"What's a latte?" the slight man asked, pronouncing it like *lat*.

"C'mon, dude. Really?" said the greasy man at the end of the line.

The woman said into her cell phone, "I'm at The Roasted Bean. It's taking forever."

"You probably don't want a latte. It has milk," Cora said.

The slight man wrung his hands. "What about a cappuccino? Does that have milk?"

"*Dude.* You can't be serious," the greasy man said.

Two people left the line and exited the coffee shop.

"It's ridiculous. Some guy can't make up his mind," the woman said into her cell phone, as if only she and the person on the other end of the line could hear. "Looks like a pedophile."

The woman had whispered the last bit, but it was still loud enough for Cora to hear.

The slight man glanced at the woman on her cell phone.

She stared at him with a look of disgust.

The slight man faced Cora again, red-faced, sweat beading on his brow.

"Do you mind if I make a suggestion?" Cora asked.

The slight man nodded.

"I personally like the house roasted vanilla bean with three organic sugars. There's no milk, and it's not a very strong coffee taste. What do you think?"

The slight man pursed his lips. "What if I don't like it?"

Cora smiled. "Then I'll buy you another coffee of your choice."

"If you will *just* order, I'll buy your freakin' coffee," the greasy man said.

The slight man smiled at Cora and said, "Okay. I'll have that."

"Thank God," said the woman on the phone.

Cora tapped on the register and sent the order to Martina to prepare. "That'll be $3.35."

The slight man reached into the front pocket of his jean shorts and dumped a pile of coins on the counter.

The greasy man laughed. "Can you believe this guy?"

The woman on the phone twisted her face and said into the phone, "Now he's paying with pennies."

Cora picked up the warm coins and threw away a piece of lint. They weren't all pennies, although there were seventeen of those. She found the total needed and handed the remaining coins back to the slight man. "Your coffee will be ready shortly." Cora gestured to the counter near Martina. "You can pick it up over there."

The slight man hesitated, then walked over to the counter by the coffeemakers.

"It's a friggin' miracle," the greasy man said.

The woman on the phone stepped up to the register.

Cora smiled and said, "Welcome to The Roasted Bean."

The woman pointed to the menu and mumbled something inaudible.

Cora leaned toward the woman. "I'm sorry, ma'am. I couldn't hear you."

The woman frowned and said into her phone, "Can you hold on?" Still with the frown, she enunciated with exaggeration. "Large iced coffee. Medium roast. House blend. Two sugars. Milk." The woman handed Cora her Discover card, then went back to her phone conversation.

The credit card machine was self-serve, so Cora had to turn the machine around to run the card for the customer.

"Sorry about that," the woman said into her cell phone. "I should've gone to Starbucks."

Cora processed the customer's credit card and turned the screen again, so the customer could sign with the stylus. "Could you sign please?" She handed the card to the woman.

The woman grabbed her credit card and signed but didn't acknowledge Cora, still busy talking on her phone. "My afternoon's crazy too." The woman then ambled toward Martina.

The greasy man stepped to the register. "It's about time."

Cora forced a smile. "I'm so sorry for the wait, sir. What can I get for you?"

The bell on the front door jingled.

"I'll have a chocolate scone and one of those vanilla coffees you like. I figure you must know." The greasy man winked at Cora.

Cora suppressed a cringe. "They are good." She processed the order and said, "That'll be $7.22."

"Whoa. That's some serious inflation. I remember when I could get coffee at Dunkin' Donuts for ninety-nine cents."

"I think you still can."

The greasy man handed Cora a ten-dollar bill.

Two new customers queued behind the greasy man.

Cora dipped her head, recognizing Troy but not the attractive blonde on his arm. She processed the greasy man's payment.

The greasy man winked again and said, "Thanks, hon." Then, he moseyed over to Martina.

Troy stepped up to the counter. He had been one year ahead of her in high school. He was tall and athletic, with boy-band hair and a face that was almost too pretty for a man.

"Welcome to the Roasted Bean," Cora said.

Troy's girlfriend stared at the menu on the wall behind Cora.

"What do you want, babe?" Troy asked his girlfriend.

"I think, like, an iced coffee with whipped cream," the blonde replied.

Troy turned from the blonde to Cora. His eyes narrowed in recognition. "Hey, ... Fivehead, what up?"

Troy was notorious for assigning nicknames that stuck. Cora's nickname had been Fivehead because of her massive forehead. Cora's face turned to stone. "Cora. My name's Cora."

Troy smirked. "Right. Sorry. I'm terrible with names."

"What do you want?"

"*Attitude*," the blonde said under her breath.

"Uh, one of those iced coffees with whipped cream," Troy said.

"What size?" Cora asked.

Troy glanced at his girlfriend. "Medium, okay?"

"Do they have a small?" the blonde asked.

"Medium's the smallest size," Cora replied.

The blonde tugged on Troy's sculpted arm. "Will you have some, if I can't finish it?"

Troy grinned at his girlfriend. "Sure, babe." Troy addressed Cora again. "Medium then."

"Is that it?" Cora asked, her tone icier than the coffee they ordered.

"No. I want a black coffee with premium blend. Large."

Cora tapped on her screen. "That'll be $6.79."

Troy slid his credit card into the machine. He signed with the stylus, and Cora handed him his receipt.

The bell on the door jingled again. Cora glanced toward the door. Mo Williams walked toward the counter, his shoulders slumped. He was tall but a little shorter than Troy and more muscular. Cora almost didn't recognize him. She was certain he wouldn't recognize her. They'd never spoken. Mo had been the most popular boy in school, if you didn't count Troy.

Troy turned from the counter and walked toward Mo. "What up, Mo?"

Mo smiled, showing bright white teeth. "Hey, Troy."

Troy replied in a lower but still audible voice, "Hey, man. I wanted to talk to you after what happened. I tried texting you, but you never responded. I feel bad. It was my *weed*."

Troy had whispered *weed*, but Cora still overheard.

"Don't worry about it," Mo replied.

"Thanks for not snitching," Troy said.

Mo broke eye contact. "Yeah."

Troy's girlfriend approached the men.

"Go wait for the coffee," Troy said to her. "I'll be there in a minute."

The blonde pivoted and walked to Martina, a frown on her face.

Troy turned back to Mo. "Bitches. You know how it is."

Mo nodded, noncommittal.

"What have you been doing? You planning to transfer to another school?"

Mo shrugged. "Yeah. Probably." Mo motioned toward the counter. "I should, uh, …"

Troy stepped aside. "Yeah, man. Get your coffee. We'll have to party this summer."

"Yeah, … cool."

Troy walked back to his girlfriend.

Mo shuffled up to Cora.

"Welcome to The Roasted Bean," Cora said. "What can I get for you?"

Mo glanced at Troy and his girlfriend. Troy was busy sweet-talking her. Mo cleared his throat and said, "An application. Could I have an application?"

Cora was stunned for an instant. "Sure. Of course." She reached under the counter and grabbed an application with a clipboard and a pen.

Mo took the application with a bowed head. "Thank you." Then, he went to a booth and sat down.

Troy and his girlfriend grabbed their coffees and walked toward the exit. They stopped at Mo's booth on the way out. Troy said, "Dude, you're trying to get a job here?"

Mo looked up from the application. "I need a job. I gotta get my dad off my ass."

"Me too. My dad wants me to intern this summer at his law firm. Dude, it's fucking boring. I got an interview for a pretty rad job though."

"Good for you."

The blonde tugged on Troy's arm. "We're going to be late for the movie."

"Later, bro," Troy said, lifting his chin to Mo.

Mo nodded back and watched the couple leave the coffee shop. Troy and his girlfriend climbed into a shiny silver Mercedes G-Wagon. They sped away. Mo removed the application from the clipboard and folded the paper twice. Then, he stood from the booth, leaving the clipboard and the pen. He hurried from the coffee shop, throwing the application away on his way out.

Cora's phone buzzed in her back pocket. It was an email notification from Total Graphic Design.

The subject read *Don't forget to download the employment portal.*

She opened the email and clicked the employment portal link. Another message appeared, asking her if she wanted to give TotalGraphicDesign.com access to her phone. This time she tapped Yes.

# Chapter 3: Mo's Big Break

The clock on Mo's bedside table read *11:11 a.m.* He climbed out of bed, not wanting his father to come home from work and find him in his pajamas again. Mo went to the bathroom, peed, and washed his hands. He flipped the switch for the vanity lights, further brightening the bathroom. He stripped and stood nude in front of the full-length mirror.

His body appeared to be the picture of health, with low body fat and ropy muscles. Mo ran his hand over every inch of his body, searching for any swelling. His chest was a collage of burn scars. The tip of his right pinkie was missing. He'd been referred to Child Protective Services several times in elementary school for suspected abuse, but his parents had never laid a hand on him. He paid special attention to his left knee and the site of his surgery scar. He checked himself in the mirror, looking for any discoloration or redness within his dark skin. Finally, he checked his mouth and teeth.

Mo dressed, went to his desk, and opened his laptop. He scanned his email, stopping to open one above the others.

From: Admin@TotalSportsAgency.com
To: MoWilliams88@gmail.com
Subject: Your Application

Dear Applicant,

Thank you for taking the time to download the employment portal for the internship program at Total Sports Agency.

According to our records, you have not completed the online application. If you would like to do that now, please click the link below.

## Online Application

Mo clicked the link and filled out the online application. After he clicked Send on the application, an automatic email appeared, informing him that he would be notified within forty-eight hours if he was chosen for an in-person interview.

\*\*\*

Later that evening, Mo sat on his bed, his laptop on his thighs, watching his high school football highlights. The quarterback threw a fade into the corner of the end zone. On-screen, Mo jumped over two defensive backs to snag the football out of the air. In another play, Mo caught a screen pass, ran over a cornerback, then outran both safeties for a ninety-two-yard touchdown.

Mo thought about the worn cartilage in his knee and the early stages of arthritis. The orthopedist had told him not to run anymore and certainly no football. The doc had said, "You should try biking." Mo wiped the corners of his eyes and paused himself on-screen—as he held out his hands, standing in the end zone, after another touchdown catch.

An email notification flashed on the corner of his laptop screen. Mo clicked on the notification.

From: Admin@TotalSportsAgency.com
To: MoWilliams88@gmail.com
Subject: Your Application

Dear Applicant,

Congratulations. Your application has been approved for an in-person interview.

Your interview is scheduled on 5-18-2021 at 10:00 a.m. at Total, LLC, 610 Lancaster Avenue, Office #52, Berwyn, PA 19312.

If you would like to attend the in-person interview, please click the link below.

### Confirm Interview

Mo clicked the link.

# Chapter 4: Mo and Total Sports Agency

The Uber driver dropped Mo in front of a six-story office building made of concrete and tinted glass. He checked the time on his phone, shielding the screen from the sun—*9:07 a.m.* He was almost an hour early, but he had planned on it, not wanting something as simple as being late to ruin his opportunity.

He entered the building, carrying pens and copies of his résumé inside his old leather briefcase. Originally, it had been his grandfather's, the serial entrepreneur who always had a great idea but had never made any money. His mother had kept it as a keepsake when he died. Mo had kept it as a keepsake when she died.

A waiting area with leather chairs, potted plants, and a few end tables sat to his right. Beyond the waiting area, a security desk and a guard blocked entry to the first-floor offices and the elevators. Mo sat in the empty waiting area, not ready yet, picking the seat in the corner, farthest away from the security desk.

He took a deep breath and closed his eyes, visualizing himself shaking hands and smiling at the interviewer. Mo imagined a crotchety old white man in a power suit, who didn't want a young black man at his company. Mo thought about the questions the interviewer might ask. He visualized himself answering with charm and intelligence, winning over the man, despite his prejudices.

Before a big football game, Mo had always imagined myriad difficult situations and how he would overcome them. A fast cornerback. An overtly physical safety who wanted to knock off Mo's helmet with his head still inside. A referee unwilling to throw a flag for pass interference, even though the defender was draped over Mo's back.

Mo didn't think he'd meet a bigoted boomer that morning, but overcoming the toughest of circumstances in his mind helped his confidence.

The elevator door dinged, causing Mo to open his eyes. A petite young man exited, his head bowed, holding a sketchbook and several folders. Mo clenched his fists, his entire body tensing. *Brian.* Mo looked away, not wanting to lose his Zen-like confidence, and definitely not wanting to alert Brian to his presence.

Mo waited for the glass front door to open and shut, before checking that Brian was gone. He was. Mo let out a deep cleansing breath and thought, *I didn't visualize that.*

# Chapter 5: Cora and Total Graphic Design

Cora approached the security guard and said, "I'm here for an interview with Total Graphic Design."

He looked up from his phone. "You mean, Total, LLC?"

"Yes."

"I'll need your name and one form of identification."

Cora gave her name and showed her license to the man. She was then allowed access to the elevators.

"Total, LLC is on the fifth floor," the security guard said. "Office number fifty-two."

Cora took the elevator to the fifth floor, then found Total, LLC. She entered the glass door, which opened into a small room. A few chairs were along the wall, and an attractive woman was seated at the reception desk. She smiled in Cora's direction. A sign affixed to the desk read Total Graphic Design.

"Welcome to Total Graphic Design," the receptionist said. "You must be Cora."

Cora smiled. *I can't believe she knows my name.* "I am. Thank you."

The receptionist gestured to the chairs along the wall. "Please have a seat. I'll let Jim know that you're here. He'll be interviewing you."

"Okay. Thank you." Cora sat on a chair, watching and listening to the receptionist.

"Your eleven o'clock is here," the receptionist said into the desktop phone. "Great. Thanks, Jim." She hung up the phone and said to Cora, "He'll be right with you."

As Cora waited, she tugged on her ill-fitting skirt suit, worried that it was riding up too high. It had been her sister's—a size two. Cora typically wore a size four.

A door opened to the waiting room, and a fit man with salt-and-pepper hair appeared. Cora stood from her seat, pulling down her skirt at the same time. The man approached with a wide smile. He held out his hand. "Hi, Cora. I'm Jim Levin, director of human resources."

Cora shook the man's hand. "It's nice to meet you."

"Likewise. Are you ready?"

"Yes. I'm excited."

"That's great. We love enthusiasm here."

Jim led Cora through the door and down a hallway. They walked past several offices, but the doors were all shut, and it was eerily quiet. At the end of the hall, a door was open. A gold placard was attached to the door with Jim's name and title. Jim led Cora inside the office, shutting the door behind them.

Cora looked at the door, her heart pounding, like a trapped animal.

Jim gestured to the chair in front of his dark wooden desk. "Please. Have a seat."

Cora sat in the leather chair, with her sketchbook and painting in her lap. She surveyed her surroundings. The office was neat, almost sterile. Jim had a laptop on the desk, with one small stack of papers, and two gold pens in an ornate wooden holder. A few framed prints were on the walls. Mostly realistic landscapes, not unlike Cora's artistic style.

Jim eyed Cora's lap.

Cora pulled down her skirt reflexively, jostling her artwork.

"I see you brought a painting," Jim said.

"Oh. Right."

"I'd love to see your work."

Cora handed Jim the small painting and her sketchbook. Jim flipped through the sketchbook for several minutes, nodding to himself, a smile on his lips. Then, he picked up the painting of a wildflower meadow, a maple tree in the background and a bright blue sky with fluffy clouds overhead.

"Beautiful," Jim said. "Just beautiful."

Cora blushed.

Jim set the artwork on the edge of his desk, near Cora. "You are obviously a very creative person."

"Thank you," Cora replied.

"I always like to see creativity because we can teach you the nuts and bolts of graphic design, but we can't teach you creativity. Either you have it or you don't. I'm happy to say you have it."

Cora smiled wide.

Jim went to the stack of papers. "It says here that you're currently working full-time at The Roasted Bean."

"That's correct," Cora replied.

"What is the best thing about working there?"

Cora paused. "Um, … it's close to my house, so I can walk."

Jim tilted his head. "Do you not have access to a car?"

"Oh, I do," Cora lied. "I just like to walk, especially when the weather's nice."

For the next thirty minutes, Jim asked Cora questions about her work history, her aspirations, and her artwork.

At the conclusion of the interview, Jim asked, "Do you have anything you'd like to ask about the position?"

"When will you decide who you are hiring?" Cora asked.

"Very soon but we have another round of interviews first."

"Another round?"

Jim nodded. "Yes. We're very thorough. Our CEO always says we should be slow to hire but quick to fire."

Cora grimaced.

"Don't worry. We rarely ever fire anyone. That's the benefit of hiring the right people in the first place. I don't want to get ahead of myself, but I think you can expect an invitation to the final interview."

# Chapter 6: Mo and The Tip

Mo checked his naked body in the full-length mirror. He thought about the interview he'd had two days ago. Mo thought it went well. The director of human resources had said, "I don't want to get ahead of myself, but I think you can expect an invitation to the final interview."

Mo checked his hands for swelling or discoloration. He stared at his right pinky finger and thought, *I don't remember biting off the tip. Why would I? Do I remember anything from back then?* After completing his daily ritual, he dressed and sat down at his laptop to check his email. He scrolled through his recent messages, his heart pounding. Then, he found what he was looking for.

From: Admin@TotalSportsAgency.com
To: MoWilliams88@gmail.com
Subject: Interview

Dear Maurice,

Congratulations. You have been selected for the final interview for the position of intern at Total Sports Agency.

Your interview is scheduled on 5-27-2021 at 10:00 a.m.

Final interviews are conducted at our country offices in Rockland, PA. This office is out of the way and difficult to find, so we will provide transportation to and from the interview.

We will send a car to your home at 9:00 a.m. on the date of the final interview.

If you would like to attend the final interview, please click the link below.

## Confirm Interview

Mo sprang from his seat and shouted, "Hell, yeah."

# Chapter 7: Cora and The Country Office

The television blared in the living room. It was on twenty-four hours per day, providing entertainment during her mother's waking hours and comfort while she slept. At 8:58 a.m., it was providing comfort, while her mother drooled on the couch cushions and snored, with decibels comparable to a circular saw. That's what her dad used to say, with a wry grin. "Sounded like you were cuttin' wood with my circular saw." That was before one of his laborers fell off a roof and never walked again. His construction company wasn't covered specifically for roofing. Bankruptcy followed. After that, Cora's family fell apart piece by piece. Cora's dad left with Crystal, a woman closer to Cora's age than her father's. Her mother fell into a metaphorical hole and tried to drag Cora and her sister with her. Cora was the only one still fighting.

Cora stared at her sleeping mother. *I can't do this anymore. It's time for me to take care of myself.* Cora left the house, shutting the door softly behind her.

A black Lincoln Town Car was parked along the curb. A man in a dark suit stood next to the rear passenger door. Cora walked toward the man, wearing the tight skirt suit she'd worn to the first interview nine days ago.

The man opened the car door. "Good morning, Ms. Hinton."

Cora forced a smile. "Good morning."

Cora gazed out the window, clutching her purse, as they drove toward Rockland. Cora hadn't mentioned the interview to her mother. She didn't want to hear any negativity, worrying that it might jinx her somehow. She thought about her sister. *She would've been jealous and snippy.* A pang of guilt settled in Cora's stomach. *My mother acts like she was a saint. Why do people do that after someone dies?* Cora swallowed hard. She reached into her purse, removed a tissue, and blotted the corners of her eyes. She fanned herself, trying to stop the tears from coming and ruining her mascara.

She grabbed her phone and opened Instagram, hoping for a distraction.

***

They had driven north for nearly an hour, the scenery more and more rural as they went. Cora looked up from her Instagram feed and asked, "Are we close?"

The driver glanced in his rearview mirror at Cora and talked for the first time since they left. "Very close."

Cora slipped her phone back into her purse and looked out the window. They drove by forests and farmland, everything bright green. They drove over a stone bridge, the creek swollen from the spring rains.

The driver turned the car onto a long driveway that wound through the forest. The hair on the back of Cora's neck stood on end. *I'm alone in the middle of nowhere with this guy. What if . . .*

After a short jaunt, they reached a clearing of neatly striped green grass, surrounding a castle-like mansion. The stone manor was Gothic and colossal, featuring five chimneys. Several luxury vehicles were parked in front. The circular driveway led them to the front portico. The driver stopped the car. A sign stood in front of the portico. *Welcome TSA, TGD, and TTA Candidates!*

Cora breathed a sigh of relief, the sign giving some legitimacy to the situation. She figured TGD stood for Total Graphic Design, but she didn't know about the other initialisms.

The driver opened the door for Cora.

She stepped out of the Lincoln onto the driveway. A solitary cloud muted the bright sun.

"We're here," the driver said, gesturing toward the portico. "Go in through the front door, and a sign will point you to the waiting area."

Cora scanned the scene. "Will you be here to take me home?"

"No, ma'am. I was told that someone else will drive you home."

Cora nodded, gawking at the front door fit for a giant. She hesitated, then walked toward the portico. An ornate knocker shaped like the face of a lion was attached to the door. She might've knocked, if not for the driver's instructions.

The Lincoln drove away.

She opened the door and stepped inside. Cora looked around, surveying the scene. Faint voices came from somewhere, but she saw no one. The walls in the foyer were bloodred, with baroque trim, and a chandelier overhead. Beyond the foyer was a stone fireplace, circular staircase, and neatly arranged antique furniture. A nearby sign featured an arrow pointing left and a message underneath. *Follow the signs to the library at the end of the hall. Your interviewer will be with you shortly.*

Cora turned left, walking down the long hallway. A few signs were placed every twenty feet or so, indicating with an arrow that she was on the correct track. A final sign stood next to the open door at the end of the hallway. *Welcome Candidates. Please wait inside the library.* Being a carpenter's daughter, she noticed the thick wooden door and heavy-duty iron hinges.

Cora walked into the library. The windowless room was dominated by dark wooden bookshelves, containing old hardbacks. The ceiling was very high. Five leather chairs were arranged in a semicircle around an Oriental rug, facing a flat-screen television that hung high over the fireplace.

A young man, who looked vaguely familiar, sat on a chair staring at the floor, his foot tapping the carpet. He reminded her of a young Ben Stiller but less cute. As Cora moved closer, she sucked in a breath. Allie Gillespie, her ex–best friend, sat on another leather chair, tapping on her cell phone.

Allie looked up and locked gazes with Cora. Allie's eyes were bright blue—or at least the colored contacts made them so. Her blond hair was highlighted and shiny, courtesy of her hairdresser. She was dressed to the nines with a designer skirt suit, pantyhose, and heels. The only blemish on her otherwise perfect presentation was a sore on her bottom lip.

Allie drew her dark eyebrows together. "Look who's here."

Cora opened her mouth, but nothing came out.

"I know you're not here for the influencer gig. Total Talent Agency?"

"Graphic design. The graphic design internship," Cora replied.

The young man chimed in. "I think this place is three companies. Total Graphic Design, Total Talent Agency, and whatever TSA is. They're probably sister companies or something."

Allie scowled at the young man. "This isn't your conversation, thank you."

"I, uh, …" The young man dipped his head.

Allie turned her scowl back to Cora.

Cora broke eye contact and sat in the leather chair farthest from Allie and next to the young man.

Mo Williams entered the library, wearing a suit and tie, and carrying an old leather briefcase. He scanned the room, his eyes settling on the budding blonde influencer. "Allie?"

"Mo? What are you doing here?" Allie asked.

Cora thought, *This is so weird. I think everyone used to go to Jefferson High. It can't be a coincidence. Maybe they're recruiting Jefferson grads?*

"I'm interviewing with Total Sports Agency," Mo said.

"Now we know what TSA is," said the young man, butting in again.

Allie gave him another dirty look.

Mo also looked at the young man with contempt.

He waved. "Hey, Mo."

"Brian." Mo sat down on the leather chair opposite Brian and set his briefcase on the floor.

Cora wondered about the briefcase. *It's such an old-man move.*

Brian addressed Mo. "I heard about what happened. ... You know, at Penn State? Tough break."

Cora thought she detected an element of glee in Brian's voice.

Mo stared back at Brian for a long beat. "Yeah." Mo turned his attention to Cora. "You work at The Roasted Bean? Right?"

Cora nodded. "I'm Cora."

"I'm Mo." He scanned the room, as if making sure nobody was watching him. "Am I the only one who thinks this whole thing is strange?"

Cora was about to agree, but then Troy sauntered into the room. She stiffened.

Troy noticed Mo first. "What up, Mo?"

Mo lifted his chin. "Troy."

Cora thought, *I should get out of here. Would they take me back without interviewing? The driver left, and I'm in the middle of nowhere.*

Allie stood from her seat and stalked to Troy. She said in a hushed whisper, "I need to talk to you, ... *alone.*"

Allie and Troy stepped away from the sitting area to the open space near the south wall. They whispered back and forth, their conversation inaudible, but Allie's expression was distressed.

Cora, Mo, and Brian all snuck occasional glances at the pair.

Allie finally said loudly, "Fuck you, Troy." Then she said to the rest of them in the sitting area, "I don't know what this is, but I'm outta here."

The heavy library door shut and latched, sealing them all inside.

# Chapter 8: Mo and No Escape

"What the hell!" Allie said, rushing to the door.

Mo stood from his chair and jogged behind her. Troy and Cora followed.

Allie pulled on the door handle, but it wouldn't budge. Then, she knocked on the door with the side of her fist. "Let me outta here! You can't keep me in here."

"Mind if I try?" Mo asked.

Allie turned to Mo. "Be my guest."

Mo grabbed the handle, pressed the latch, and pulled, but it didn't budge. He tried pushing too, thinking that it would be embarrassing if it opened, but that didn't work either. He banged on the door. "Hey. Open up!"

Cora and Troy watched, a few feet away, not sure what to do.

Brian joined the group and said, "Someone's on the flat screen."

Mo and everyone else turned to the flat screen at the opposite end of the library.

A dark figure in a hoodie was on-screen. It was too dark to discern any facial features. "Please sit down," the dark figure said, with a digitized voice.

Everyone left the door for the flat screen hanging over the fireplace.

Allie glared at the screen, talking with exaggerated hand movements. "What the hell's going on? Why's the door locked?"

"Your questions will be answered when the time is right. In the meantime, we must commence with the interviews."

"You need to let me out. I'm not doing this," Mo said, his arms crossed over his chest.

"I think that's a mistake. You all have much to gain," the figure replied.

Mo went back to the door. He crouched and slammed his shoulder into the door, but it didn't budge.

The rest of the group joined Mo at the door.

The digitized voice said, "Please come back. I'll make it worth your while."

Mo looked at an audio speaker in the ceiling. "Open this door, or I'm calling the police."

The voice didn't respond.

Mo grabbed his phone from his pocket.

Allie said, "I don't have any cell service or internet."

Mo turned from the door to see everyone checking their phones. Mo looked at his phone too. No service. "Shit."

"I had service earlier," Cora said.

"So did I," Allie said.

"He must be jamming our phones or something," Brian said.

"This is so crazy," Cora said.

Troy approached Mo and the locked door. He kicked the door, but again it didn't budge. Troy sneered at a speaker in the ceiling. "If you don't let us out, we'll fucking destroy this house."

"There are only two choices," the voice said. "You can interview, or you can stay locked up. It's your choice."

"I'm getting out of here," Mo said.

"Me too," Troy replied.

"Please let me know when you're ready for the interviews," the voice said.

Mo and Troy removed their suit jackets and tried ramming the door together, but that didn't work. The group scoured the library for a way out or for anything that might help them escape, but they found nothing helpful. They tried ramming the door again, this time with all three guys, but the door still didn't budge.

The group went back to the screen.

"What do you want from us?" Mo asked.

"*Honesty*," the dark figure replied. "In return, you will be well compensated."

A panel in the high ceiling slid open a crack, the size of a mailbox slit. One-hundred-dollar bills rained from the ceiling.

# Chapter 9: Cora and Betrayal

"They're hundred-dollar bills," Brian said, picking up one, then another.

"There's one thousand dollars," the dark figure said. "Everyone, please take two hundred dollars for your trouble."

Cora picked up two of the one-hundred-dollar bills, along with the rest of the group.

"Now open the door," Mo said, scowling at the flat screen.

"We must have the interviews first," the dark figure replied. "By accepting the money, you are all consenting to the interview process."

Mo tossed his cash on the floor. "Let me out. I don't want your money."

"It's too late for that." The dark figure hesitated for a second. "Raise your hand if you've ever done something terrible to another person."

Cora thought about what she did to Allie.

The group eyed each other, but nobody raised their hand.

"Remember. This is about honesty," the dark figure said.

Cora raised her hand.

"Thank you for your honesty, Cora." Two more hundred-dollar bills fell from the slit in the ceiling. "Please collect your reward."

Cora picked up her money and shoved it into her purse. She picked up Mo's money too and held it out to him.

"I don't want it," Mo said.

"I'll take it," Troy said.

Cora shoved the extra $200 into her purse and said to Mo, "I'll hold it for you."

"Anyone else?" the dark figure asked.

Nobody raised their hand.

The dark figure let out a heavy breath. "If you can't be honest, you can't work here."

Brian raised his hand.

Mo glared at Brian.

"That's good, Brian," the dark figure said.

Brian peered up at the ceiling for his money.

"No reward for you, Brian. You took too long. Fortune favors the bold. The early adopters. The truly brave." The dark figure paused for an instant, then said, "Raise your hand if you dislike someone in this room."

Cora cast a side-eyed glance at Troy and then Allie. The group eyed each other again, but nobody raised their hand.

"Don't be shy. There's a reward for being honest."

Allie raised her hand, glowering at Cora.

Three hundred dollars fell from the slit in the ceiling.

"Thank you, Allie. Please collect your reward," the dark figure said.

Allie picked up her money.

"Anyone else?"

Cora raised her hand, giving Allie a dirty look. She waited for the money, but nothing came.

"Sorry, Cora. Remember. The reward is for the first to act, the truly bold, the true originals. No rewards for sheep. It's interesting that the two women are the only ones with the balls to admit that they dislike someone. Females often settle their disputes with gossip and manipulation, but men are much more likely to settle their disputes with physical violence. I think this makes women so arrogant. You know what I'm talking about, don't you, guys? A female talks trash to some guy, and it's always the boyfriend who gets beat up. Well, not today. Here at Total, LLC, we are all for equality. The first person to slap a female will get $400."

"That's crazy," Cora said.

"That's not an interview. That's assault," Mo said, his muscled arms crossed over his chest.

"Five hundred dollars," the dark figure said.

Nobody moved, but Allie eyed Cora, her hands twitchy.

"Six hundred dollars, ... seven hundred. Remember. The first one to connect receives the money. Eight hundred dollars, ... nine hundred. One thousand dollars."

Cora and Allie eyed each other. Allie turned away, and Cora breathed a sigh of relief.

"Two thousand dollars."

Allie wheeled around and smacked Cora across the face.

Cora shrunk back, her left cheek on fire. "Ow! Why'd you do that?"

"You know why, bitch," Allie replied.

Cora held her hand to her cheek. "He was a teacher."

"Fuck you. I loved him, and you ruined it."

"Oh, shit. You were banging a teacher?" Troy asked, his eyes like saucers. "Had to be Mr. Fitz. Am I right?"

Allie shot Troy an evil look. "Shut up, Troy."

Troy was right. It was Mr. Fitz. He was Cora's and Allie's advanced English teacher their senior year. He was fired and moved to the West Coast to escape the scandal.

"I didn't mean to ..." Cora trailed off.

"To what?" Allie clenched her fists.

Cora shrugged. "I don't know—"

"You ruined my life." Allie blitzed Cora, her fist cocked for a punch this time.

Cora cowered and covered her head, bracing for impact.

Mo intervened, grabbing Allie around the waist and holding her back. "Leave her alone."

"Let me go!" Allie said, wiggling in his grasp.

"Calm down, and I'll let go," Mo replied.

Allie stopped struggling, her breathing elevated. "Fine. I won't touch her."

Mo let go but stood between the two young women.

Cora stood upright. "You stole every guy I ever loved."

Allie cackled. "You've never even had a serious boyfriend, unless you count the Dexter Lucas disaster."

Cora blushed. "Because you stole them before we even had a chance. Remember Zach?"

The former friends went back and forth with barely a breath, while the young men served as the audience.

Allie put her hands on her hips. "Zach who?"

"Zach Branson," Cora replied.

"From middle school? You can't be serious."

Cora narrowed her eyes. "You knew I liked him. That's the only reason you went after him."

Allie lifted one shoulder. "I did you a favor. He was a terrible kisser with those braces."

Troy laughed.

"What about Jake Quinn?" Cora asked.

"He wasn't your boyfriend either," Allie replied.

Cora clenched her fists. "I was in love with him, and you knew it."

"He didn't even know you were alive."

"That's not true." Cora sounded whiny. "Remember that Fourth of July party at your house?"

Allie shrugged.

"We were talking, and you swooped in, like you always do. Kissed him with tongue and everything. Remember that?"

"That's fucked up," Troy said, grinning.

Allie pointed at Troy. "Shut the fuck up, Troy." She addressed Cora again. "That was another favor. He was a fucking loser, but I was your best friend, and you stabbed me in the back."

Cora dipped her head.

One-hundred-dollar bills rained from the ceiling.

Allie collected her money, like a stripper after a pole dance.

# Chapter 10: Mo and Dreams

"Very good, Allie," the dark figure said. "I love your passion. You'll need that passion to succeed as an Instagram influencer."

Allie shoved her wad of cash into her purse. Then she scowled at the screen. "I did what you want. Now let me the fuck outta here."

"That's not how the interviews work. We need to see more, before deciding whether you're Total material. To show that I'm not sexist, the next challenge is to punch a man in this room. The first person to punch a man will receive $3,000."

Mo addressed the flat screen. "We're not playing your game anymore." Then, he addressed the group. "I think we're in danger. This isn't random. Most of us know each other. Someone's fucking with us."

"Yes," the dark figure said. "We like our young recruits to know each other. We find that this allows for better group cohesion, and we see you with your interview mask removed. We get the chance to see who you really are in various situations. We're looking for bold go-getters, who will be loyal to the Total brand."

"You can't keep us in here forever," Troy said to the dark figure. "My dad owns a law firm. I'll own Total brands by the time this is over."

The dark figure cackled. "I have no intention of keeping you in here. The interviews will eventually conclude, with or without your consent or your daddy's law firm. Your threats have no teeth here."

Troy crossed his arms over his chest. "We'll see about that."

The dark figure let out a digitized sigh. "Troy, Troy, Troy. I had such high hopes for you. The fact that you're threatening me with your daddy's law firm is precisely your problem. You think you can do anything you want to people without consequences. Don't you?"

Troy furrowed his brow. "What the hell are you talking about?"

"Maybe it's better if I show you. Allie, you should pay special attention to this."

The dark figure disappeared from the screen, replaced by a text string.

**Lisa**: I'm freaking out! My doctor said I have herpes

**Troy**: Sucks. How is that my problem?

**Lisa**: U GAVE IT TO ME ASSHOLE

**Troy**: I don't know what ur talking about. I'm clean. I'm lucky I didn't get it from ur nasty pussy.

**Lisa**: U FUCKIN LIAR. I know u gave it to Megan Jacobs

Troy glowered at the screen, his face blazing red. "How the fuck did you get into my phone?" Troy wasn't ready for Allie's straight right. Her fist connected with Troy's nose, sending him staggering back two steps, holding his face. "God damn it, Allie." Troy stood up straight and wiped at his nose. Blood stained the side of his finger.

Allie backed away from Troy. "You're a liar, Troy. I knew something was wrong. Look at my fucking face."

Three thousand dollars rained from the ceiling.

The dark figure chuckled and reappeared on the flat screen. "You really do have what it takes to be a star, Allie. You'll have to get some Valtrex for that sore to be camera ready, but you definitely have what it takes to be a star."

Allie sneered at the dark figure. "Fuck you."

"I suggest you collect your money."

Allie hesitated, then bent down and scooped up the bills.

Brian picked up a few errant bills.

"Give it to me," Allie shrieked, holding out her hand.

Brian handed the bills to Allie. "I was just helping you. *Jeez.*"

"Herpes is forever. There's no cure. Did you know that?" the dark figure asked.

Allie shoved wads of cash into her purse, sniffling. Tears streaked down her cheeks, carrying bits of dark mascara. She stood and glared at Troy. "You ruined me. You *asshole.*"

"I didn't do shit, bitch," Troy said. "I'm the one who needs to get checked out. You probably gave it to me."

Allie rushed Troy, but he was ready this time and pushed her, knocking her off balance. One of her spiky heels snapped, and she fell to the floor.

Cora knelt next to Allie and put her arm around her. Allie cried on her shoulder.

The room was silent for several minutes, except for the sound of Allie sobbing. Cora gave Allie a pack of tissues from her purse. Allie wiped her face, slipped off her heels, and stood, with the help of Cora.

Mo said, "He—I think it's a *he*—is trying to divide us. This guy's been stalking us. He probably knows us."

"The employment portal!" Brian said. "It must've been malware."

"Brian's right. He probably has access to our phones and computers, whatever we used to download that portal." Mo rubbed his head from back to front and blew out a breath. "We need to stop listening to him and start figuring out a way to get out of here. Whatever beef we have between us, we need to set it aside, until we get out of here."

"Mo's right," Brian replied. "We need to work together."

"It's interesting that Mo and Brian are playing the mediators," the dark figure said. "They're all about unity and working together, right? I wonder. ... Was this unity?"

Video of a high school football intrasquad scrimmage appeared on the screen. Everyone watched Mo streaking past a short white cornerback. The pass was perfect, delivered by number twelve, Troy Pennington. Mo caught it in stride. Touchdown.

"Look at that pass," Troy said. "Damn, I should be playing college ball."

After the play, Mo held the football out to the roasted cornerback, Mo's helmet going up and down, as he added insult to injury with a little trash talk.

The video showed another play. Mo caught a screen pass from Troy. Then, Mo ran over the little cornerback, knocking him flat on his back. His teammates went wild, as Mo sprinted for another touchdown. On the way back to the sideline, Mo pointed and said something to the cornerback, who hung his head and slumped his shoulders.

"That kid, number twenty-five, got trucked," Troy said. "Damn, he sucked."

Mo shook his head at Troy.

The dark figure appeared again and said, "Correct me if I'm wrong, but wasn't that you playing cornerback, Brian?"

Brian didn't respond.

"What did Mo say to you?" the dark figure asked.

Brian shrugged. "I don't remember." His eyes were glassy.

"I find that difficult to believe. You're crying."

Brian wiped his eyes with the sleeve of his button-down shirt.

"I'll give you $500 to tell us what he said."

Brian glanced at Mo, then looked at the screen. "It was just trash talk. He was good, and he told everyone all the time how great he was." Brian looked up at the ceiling, expecting the money.

"If you want it to rain, Brian, we need specifics," the dark figure said.

"He said that I sucked and that it was too easy for him. He called me Toast, said it was because he was always burning me, like burnt toast."

Five one-hundred-dollar bills dropped from the ceiling.

The dark figure chuckled. "That must've been a reality check."

The dark figure disappeared from the screen, replaced by a freshman football program, showing a baby-faced Brian. He was listed at five foot six and 120 pounds. Each player answered the question, *What do I want to be when I grow up?* Under Brian's image it read *Professional football player*.

The dark figure appeared again. "That scrimmage, when Mo nicknamed you Toast, must've crushed your dreams."

Brian looked down.

"You must've been angry and looking for revenge. The next week at practice, you got even, didn't you?"

Mo mean-mugged Brian, thinking about the supposed accident in practice that tore his ACL. The same knee that he injured again at Penn State. The same knee that was pre-arthritic. The same knee he wasn't supposed to run on for the rest of his life.

Brian still stared at the floor.

Mo clenched his fists and moved closer to Brian. "It wasn't an accident, was it?"

Brian looked up, his face blotchy. "I slipped. It was an accident."

Mo grabbed Brian by the collar and pulled him close. "Bullshit. You did it on purpose. Didn't you?"

"Please. No. I didn't …"

Mo reared back, his fist cocked and ready. "Tell the *truth*."

Brian burst into tears. "I'm sorry, Mo. I'm sorry. I wish I could take it back."

Mo let go of Brian's collar and shoved him to the ground. Mo looked down on the former cornerback. "The NFL was my dream too. You fucking took that from me."

# Chapter 11: Mo's Got Ups

Brian cowered on the ground, expecting Mo to pummel him.

"You're not worth it." Mo turned from Brian and glowered at the dark figure on the flat screen. "Who are you? You're somebody we know, aren't you?"

"I'm the CEO of Total, LLC, Gabriel Calloway."

"Bullshit," Mo snapped. "I'm gonna find out who you are, and I'm gonna fuck you up."

The dark figure clapped. "The mask finally comes off to reveal the angry black man."

Troy appeared at Mo's side. "I want a piece of this asshole too."

The dark figure cackled. "I think Troy should worry more about Mo." The dark figure on the screen disappeared, replaced by a cell phone call log, with a date and time stamp. "Recognize that date, Mo?"

Mo gaped at the call log for a moment, processing the information. It was a call to the Penn State University Police. He turned to Troy, his fists clenched. "That's your cell phone number. It was *you*."

Troy stepped back. "Dude. That's fake. That's totally fake."

"Fuck!" Mo turned around and paced away from Troy.

Troy followed, showing his palms in surrender. "He's lying. He's trying to divide us. Didn't you say that?"

Mo whipped around and threw a right cross, connecting with Troy's jaw, dropping him like a sack of potatoes. Troy fell awkwardly, as if he had lost all motor functions, his head bouncing off the Oriental rug.

The dark figure appeared again and clapped. "One punch. Impressive."

Mo pointed at the screen. "You're next."

Nobody attended to Troy. After a few seconds he stirred and sat up. He held his chin in his hand, clicking his jaw back and forth. Troy struggled to his feet, his legs wobbly, staring at Mo with narrowed eyes. "This is fucked up, Mo. I never did shit to you."

Mo shook his head, his fists still clenched. "Bullshit. When you saw that text message from earlier, you said, 'How did you get my phone?' You were the only person who knew I had that weed. I can't believe I didn't see it before. You're lucky I don't kill you, motherfucker."

Troy shook his head. "You're wrong, man."

"Fuck you." Mo turned from Troy and looked up at the screen.

"You have every right to be angry," the dark figure said.

Mo moved the leather chair at the top of the semicircle of chairs to clear a path to the flat screen. Then, he marched to the south wall and turned around, facing the dark figure on the screen again. Mo gestured with his hands to the group, as if directing traffic. "Move out of my way."

The group backed away from the screen, clearing the way for Mo.

"Whatever it is that you think you're doing, you should stop," the dark figure said.

Mo bent down in a sprinter stance and exploded forward across the room. A few steps before he reached the north wall and the flat screen, he jumped several feet into the air, climbing the fireplace and the vertical wall with his momentum, then grabbing the top edge of the flat-screen television. Mo hung on the television, like a basketball rim, and the plastic wall mount cracked and snapped, sending the television and Mo back to Earth. Mo landed on his feet, and the television crashed to the floor, facedown, the screen shattering.

The group was wide-eyed. A few gasped at the wreckage.

Mo looked up at a ceiling-mounted speaker. "We're not playing your fucking games anymore. If you want a piece of me, come down here and show yourself."

No response came from the speakers in the ceiling.

"Now what?" Allie asked.

# Chapter 12: Cora and Dexter Lucas

Cora surveyed the room, staring at the west wall. It was the only wall without built-in bookshelves. "I have an idea." She walked to the wall and tapped on it.

"What is it?" Allie asked, following Cora.

The rest of the group followed too.

"This is drywall," Cora said. "We can break through this wall."

"How do you know that?" Mo asked.

"My dad had a construction business." Cora tapped on the wall again. "I just have to find the studs." She found two solid taps about sixteen inches apart. She touched the center, between the two studs. "I need someone to kick right here."

Mo moved into position. Cora removed her hand, and Mo kicked a hole through the drywall. Mo and Cora removed drywall with their hands, widening the hole to the studs. Mo reached for the pink insulation.

"Don't touch the insulation," Cora said.

Mo stopped short of the fluffy pink insulation.

"It's made of small fibers of glass that can irritate your eyes and skin."

Cora removed her suit jacket, using it to protect her hands, and she pulled the pink insulation from the wall cavity. Behind the insulation was the back of a stone wall. "Shit. We're not getting out through this wall. This must be an exterior wall."

Mo frowned. The others looked disappointed.

Cora scanned the room, then motioned to the east wall. "That bookcase. Behind that is an interior wall. It won't have stone behind it."

Everyone gazed at the thick wooden bookcase.

"That's some thick-ass wood," Mo said.

"We need some tools," Cora replied.

"We should search this place again." Brian scanned the room. "We didn't really check the bookshelves."

Mo nodded to Brian. "I agree. We should turn this place upside down."

Mo and Brian searched the bookshelves on the east wall, clearing books, and dumping them on the floor.

Cora and Allie worked on the south wall. Troy sat on a leather chair, brooding, seeming to accept his role as *persona non grata*.

Cora kicked off her heels and climbed the bookcase to reach the upper shelves. She tossed books down to Allie. A picture frame with a generic photo sat on the top shelf. Cora tossed it to the floor, revealing a bit of metal that glinted in the artificial light. She reached for the object, grabbing it, and pulled it into the light. "I found a pocketknife," Cora called out.

Troy stood from his seat and walked to the south wall, eyeing Cora as she climbed down with the closed pocketknife in hand. The group, including Troy, huddled around her.

Cora said, "I don't know if this will cut through the wood, but we could try."

"Give it to me," Troy said, snatching the knife from Cora. "Let me try."

"Hey," Cora said, glaring at Troy.

"I'm stronger than you are."

"You're not keeping that," Mo said.

"Fuck you, Mo," Troy said, as he opened the blade.

Mo shot Troy a look that could kill.

Troy pointed the knife at Mo, holding his gaze for a moment. Then, Troy pivoted and walked to the bookcase.

The group followed.

Troy plunged the blade into the wood, working the blade around in a circle, trying to make a hole. "This won't do shit." Troy closed the pocketknife and shoved it into his pocket.

"Give it back to Cora," Allie said.

Troy shrugged. "Someone has to hold it. What difference does it make? We're not cutting through that wood anyway."

Cora tapped on the heavy wooden bookshelf. "I hate to say it, but he's right."

The mail slot in the ceiling opened, and five sheets of paper floated to the floor. Cora and everyone else grabbed a sheet. Each was identical, with text messages and a picture.

Cora cringed when she recognized herself in the picture. Her heart thumped as she read the text string between Troy and Dexter. Dexter Lucas had been Cora's first and only boyfriend, or at least that's what he'd told her, but it had ended in humiliation.

**Troy**: Dude. Saw u in the hall today with Fivehead. Is she your girlfriend?

**Dexter**: Jus hooking up

**Troy**: Gotta do her doggy. Her face is jacked

**Dexter**: Haha

**Troy**: U fuck her yet? Heard she was a tight ass virgin

**Dexter**: I fucked her

**Troy**: Dude. You're a liar. I bet u never even seen her tits

**Dexter**: PIC

Dexter attached a nude selfie of Cora, biting her lower lip, a blush across her face.

**Troy**: Nice!

Cora stalked to Troy and tried to slap him across the face, but he grabbed her by the wrist and shoved her backward. She stumbled but maintained her balance.

"Get the fuck away from me, Fivehead," Troy said.

"You fucking asshole," Cora said, vibrating with rage. "You sent it everywhere!"

Allie shook her head, glowering at Troy. "You're a fucking asshole."

Troy frowned. "Don't get all hysterical. I didn't do anything. Dexter sent it to me. It wasn't hot enough to share."

Mo balled up the piece of paper. "You really are an asshole."

Brian balled up his page too.

"This isn't my fault," Troy said.

"I'm starting to think everything is your fault," Mo replied.

# Chapter 13: Cora and Emily

Allie collected all the pages with Cora's nude selfie, snatching one from Troy, the others handing them over willingly. Allie ripped them into tiny pieces. Cora sat on a leather chair, her head hanging.

Troy sat on the leather chair farthest from Cora. He cut through the leather armrests with the pocketknife, exposing the chair's insides.

Mo approached Cora. "Don't worry about it."

Allie approached her too. "They're all gone. I ripped them into a million pieces."

Cora sniffled and nodded.

Brian sidled up to the group. "He's a piece of shit."

"Fuck you guys," Troy said. "I can hear you."

Allie shot Troy a dirty look. "Nobody gives a shit if you can hear."

"This is what *he* wants," Mo said, gesturing to the ceiling with his chin. "We have to stay calm and figure this out." Mo addressed Cora. "Where did you find that pocketknife exactly?"

Cora looked up. "It was on the top shelf behind a picture frame."

"We haven't checked *that* top shelf yet," Brian said, pointing up at the bookshelf spanning the east wall.

Mo and Brian climbed the bookshelf to the top. They tossed books and picture frames to the floor. Cora and Allie checked the books and picture frames, in case something was hidden inside them. Troy watched from his seat, still stabbing the leather with the pocketknife.

Mo reached behind a picture frame. "There's nothing."

Brian did the same. He grabbed something. "Holy shit! It's a gun."

Allie gasped.

Cora said, "Oh, my God."

Troy rose to his feet and approached the scene.

Brian and Mo climbed down, Brian holding a shiny silver revolver. As soon as they touched the floor, five sheets of paper floated from the ceiling mail slot.

Cora and everyone else picked up one. They congregated in the middle of the Oriental rug, surrounded by the five leather chairs. Like the last mail drop, each copy was identical to the others. Cora recognized the text messages immediately.

> **Cora**: Emily is REALLY upset. She is talking about telling her parents.
>
> **Allie**: She won't tell. What would she say? I got wasted and had sex like a big fat slut
>
> **Cora**: U shouldn't have given her those pills.
>
> **Allie**: She needed to loosen up. She is so boring
>
> **Cora**: She has never been drunk before. She was in bad shape. I think she was a virgin. I'm not even sure she was awake when it happened. This is REALLY BAD.
>
> **Allie**: Better she learns how to hold her booze now than in college. How embarrassing
>
> **Cora**: This could be serious.
>
> **Allie**: Relax. U worry too much
>
> **Cora**: What about her bf?

**Allie**: She has a bf?

**Cora**: Idk, but she said his name is Brian.

Cora's stomach lurched. She looked up from the page to Brian.

Brian's jaw was set tight. His entire body was taut. He pointed the revolver at Allie, then Cora, and back again.

"Whoa, Brian," Mo said, standing to Brian's right.

Cora and Allie raised their hands, their eyes bulging.

"Who did it?" Brian said through gritted teeth.

"Did what?" Allie asked, her hands trembling.

"Who *raped* Emily?"

Allie spoke rapidly. "Everyone was wasted, but *nobody* raped anyone. I swear. I don't know for sure if Emily even had sex."

"Brian, put the gun down," Mo said. "Don't do something you'll regret."

"Shut up, Mo." Brian waved the revolver at Mo, then back to Allie. "*Who* did it?"

"Nobody *did* anything," Allie said.

An iPad with a protective case dropped from the ceiling, landing on one of the leather chairs with a *thump*.

# Chapter 14: Mo and Raising the Stakes

Brian gestured with his chin to Mo. "Pick it up, and bring it here."

Mo stepped tentatively to the leather chair, picked up the iPad as if it might be a bomb, then turned it over. A yellow sticky note was on the screen. It read *Play me.*

Brian glanced back at Mo, his gun still on Allie and Cora, with Troy behind the women. "What does it say?"

"It says, Play Me," Mo replied.

"Bring it here."

Troy crept to the right, attempting to exit the line of fire.

Brian aimed the revolver at Troy and said, "Stop."

Troy froze in his tracks and pivoted to Brian.

"Where do you think you're going?"

"Just getting out of the way. I'd rather not get shot," Troy replied.

Brian aimed the gun at Troy. "Put your hands up and stand next to Allie."

Troy didn't move. "What the fuck, man? I don't have anything to do with this."

Brian narrowed his eyes, the revolver still trained on Troy. "I don't know that. Move."

Troy raised his hands and walked over to Allie and Cora, Brian following Troy with the revolver.

"This is dangerous, Brian," Mo said, holding the iPad, and standing a safe distance behind Brian. "Why don't you put the gun down?"

Brian glanced over his shoulder. "Bring me the iPad."

"This isn't a good idea."

Brian pivoted and turned the gun on Mo. "Bring it here!"

Mo walked to Brian.

"Play it. Hold it up so I can see it."

"This isn't—"

"Play it!"

Mo removed the sticky note and pressed the button, waking the iPad. He played the video on the screen, holding it up to Brian. From their position, only Brian and Mo could see the video.

Brian still held the gun, vaguely aimed at Cora, Allie, and Troy. The video started with a man setting an iPhone camera on a dresser, pointed at a disheveled bed. Only his body was in frame. He wore jeans and a dark hoodie. The room was dark too, but a young woman was clearly visible on the bed. She was immobile. Tears filled Brian's eyes. He wiped them with his sleeve.

The man went to the bed, his back to the camera. He removed her sneakers. He unbuttoned her tight jeans and unzipped her zipper. She didn't move. He slid his hand down her pants, rubbing her crotch for a few seconds. Then, he removed her blouse and bra. He stood over her and grabbed her breasts, squeezing and batting them like they were toys. The young woman didn't move a muscle.

Brian clenched his jaw, his body shaking.

Mo looked at Brian's trigger finger, also shaking. "We should stop this," Mo said, still holding up the iPad.

Brian spoke through gritted teeth. "No."

"What's happening?" Cora asked.

Nobody answered Cora's question.

The man removed the woman's tight jeans and underwear, pulling them off her body together, her clothes coming off inside out. The man stood with his back to the camera, his hands on his hips, leering at the nude woman for a long moment. Then, it was like the man was on fire. He removed his sneakers, jeans, and underwear in a flash, his white ass in full view of the camera. He spat on his hand and rubbed his saliva on the woman's vagina.

Tears streamed down Brian's cheeks. "Show your face, you sick fuck."

The man grabbed her legs and pinned them on his shoulders. The young woman was like a ragdoll, her head lolled to the side.

Mo winced and turned away.

"What's happening?" Cora asked.

For the next thirty seconds, Mo stared at the floor.

Brian was short of breath, nearly hyperventilating.

Mo turned his head to check on Brian. His face was a blotchy, tear-streaked mess. His body trembled. Mo caught another glimpse of the screen. Thankfully, it appeared to be over. The man was close to the camera now, only the lower part of his hoodie in view. Then, the man bent down to the camera and smiled.

Brian pushed the iPad out of his line of sight, stalked closer to Troy, and fired at point-blank range.

The *pop* from the revolver reverberated throughout the room.

Allie and Cora screamed.

Troy fell to his knees and cowered, covering his head, also screaming.

Mo dropped the iPad and bent down, covering his ears.

Brian aimed the revolver at Troy and fired over and over again, until the revolver clicked, and nothing happened.

Allie and Cora crawled behind a leather chair, hugging each other.

Mo approached Brian cautiously. Troy lay on the ground, frantically checking his body for holes.

"It's over," Mo said, taking the revolver from Brian's hand, and standing between Brian and Troy.

Brian hung his head and wiped his face with the sleeve of his button-down shirt.

Mo opened the cylinder of the revolver. "I think these are blanks."

Troy rose to his feet. The crotch of his gray dress pants was wet with urine. Cora and Allie emerged from behind a leather chair.

"That motherfucker tried to kill me," Troy said, gesticulating at Brian.

"Shut the fuck up. You're a rapist." Mo shut the cylinder and placed the revolver in his pocket.

"Did it show Troy?" Cora asked.

Mo nodded to Cora.

"You're sick in the head," Allie said to Troy.

Brian sucked back mucus and glared at Allie. "It's your fault too. You got Emily all messed up."

Allie opened her mouth to speak, but nothing came out.

Mo shook his head at Allie.

Brian pointed at Troy. "When we get out of here, you're going to prison for rape."

"Fuck you. You're going to prison for attempted murder," Troy replied, walking around the group toward the iPad on the floor.

"I don't care," Brian replied, pivoting and following Troy with his gaze.

Troy smashed the iPad with the heel of his dress shoe.

"Go ahead and destroy it," Brian said. "I already saw it. Mo saw it. You're fucking guilty."

The digitized voice came from the speakers in the ceiling. "Maybe you're all guilty. I'm not sure if any of you are Total material. I don't think the normal interview process will work."

Everyone gaped at the ceiling.

"What the fuck is he talking about?" Allie asked the group.

"I need to raise the stakes to see who you really are," the voice began. "Let's play a game. Before sunrise, one of you must die. Who dies and who does the killing is entirely up to you."

Brian mean-mugged Troy, likely thinking Troy should be the first to go.

The voice continued. "Each sunrise after that, someone else must die, until there is one. As an added bonus, one deserving person will walk out of here with two million dollars."

Money fell from the ceiling. Bound stacks of one-hundred-dollar bills thumped the floor and the furniture. One stack hit Mo on top of his head. He reached down and picked it up. He flipped through the crisp bills, guessing it was probably $10,000 per bound stack. The stacks kept falling at their feet.

Mo gaped at the money. *Two million dollars in cash.*

Allie, Cora, Brian, and Troy picked up stacks of cash, their pockets and hands flush with money.

Mo broke from his trance and glared at everyone. "Leave the money alone!"

Everyone but Troy stopped and stood, red-faced, double-fisting ten-thousand-dollar stacks.

Mo looked up at the ceiling. "This is *over*. Whatever sick game you think you're playing, it's over. We're not playing. You can keep your fucking money. It's not worth killing over."

Troy stacked cash on an empty bookshelf. "Speak for yourself. This cash is mine."

The voice cackled. "Does anyone know the difference between a problem and a predicament?" The voice paused for an answer that never came. "A problem has a solution. Predicaments only have outcomes. You five are in a predicament. Someone will die each night, whether anyone participates or not. Either you choose or I choose. Of course, if I choose, you may not like the outcome. Good luck."

"He's bluffing," Mo said. "This is bullshit. Nobody's killing anyone. He can come down here and try it, but we're not doing it."

A sliver of the ceiling opened, and a rifle barrel pointed at them. A deafening *pop* came. The bullet snapped over Mo's head and hit the wall behind him.

Everyone gasped and ducked. Allie hid behind a chair.

The ceiling panel shut again. The smell of sweet charcoal and sulfur hung in the air.

The voice said, "If I wanted to kill you, you'd be dead. I assure you that I can and will kill someone at sunrise if you don't do it yourselves. You choose or I choose."

# Chapter 15: Mo and Who?

Allie rose from her hiding place behind a chair. "What the hell are we going to do? He'll kill us all."

"We have to get out of here," Cora said, standing.

Troy continued to stack cash on a bookshelf, hoarding the majority of the money.

"Nobody's killing anyone," Mo said.

"Troy deserves to die," Brian said, eyeing Troy.

Troy flipped open his knife and pivoted toward Brian and the group. "Anyone comes near me, or my money, I'll slice their fucking throat."

"He shouldn't have that knife. Nobody else has a weapon," Cora said.

"Fuck you, Fivehead. Brian tried to kill me," Troy said.

"You raped Emily, you sick fuck," Brian said, his fists clenched.

Troy lifted one side of his mouth in contempt. "She wanted it. Told me before she passed out. It's not my fault she didn't want your little dick."

Brian rushed Troy, his fist reared back.

Mo sprinted between the two, grabbing Brian and holding him back. Brian struggled against Mo, but Mo held him tight, and said, "Don't do it. This is what he wants."

Brian stopped struggling. "Let me go."

Mo let go, standing between Brian and Troy.

Brian sneered at Troy, his nostrils flaring.

Troy smirked back, holding up the pocketknife.

Mo scanned the group. "We need to set aside our issues and try to figure this out."

"Mo's right," Cora said.

Mo walked over to the wall, where the bullet likely entered, after snapping over his head. He found the bullet hole, touched it, and turned to the group. "That last shot was real. That wasn't a blank. He could've killed me. He'll kill us all if we don't work together."

Mo, Cora, Allie, and Brian congregated in the middle of the room on the Oriental rug. Troy stayed by the east wall bookcase, guarding his loot.

"He obviously wants us to kill each other," Cora said. "The question is why? Who is this person?"

"He has to be someone who we all know," Mo said.

"Maybe he thinks we all did something to him," Allie said.

"He has to be smart and good with computers," Brian said.

"This is good," Mo said. "So, someone we all know. Someone who we all hurt in some way. Someone who's smart and knows computers."

"Seems like a dude," Troy called out from his spot.

Mo nodded at Troy. "I agree. Probably a male. I think he must have money too, or his family's rich. This place is no joke. Anybody know anyone who fits this description?"

"What about Bitch Tits? What was his name?" Troy looked to Mo. "Remember that punk-ass kid who came out for football a few years ago? Short and fat with those big bitch titties."

Mo shrugged. "I don't know who you're talking about."

Brian glowered at Troy. "Greg Tomlinson. His name's Greg Tomlinson."

"You know him?" Mo asked.

Brian nodded.

"Is he smart?"

Brian nodded again. "Good with computers too but it's not him."

"How do you know that?"

"He doesn't have any money. His family's poor." Brian shot Troy a look that could kill. "Not that you care, but he lost weight. He's on an academic scholarship at UVA."

"What about that creepy kid who called in the bomb threat senior year?" Allie asked, her hands on her hips. "What was his name?"

"Jordan Young," Cora replied. "He lives on my street."

"Forget that then. He must be poor."

Cora frowned at Allie. "Yeah. He must be."

"What about that kid who got caught masturbating in class?" Allie asked.

"Blake something," Cora replied.

"Blake Lovett," Brian said. "He was special ed."

"I think we're looking at this the wrong way," Mo said. "It has to be someone that each of us hurt really bad. Think about the worst thing you've ever done to someone, and then say their name."

Mo thought about a one-night stand he'd had last year. She was two years younger than him. Sixteen when he was eighteen. He didn't know anything about her, other than she was cute and was all over him at that party. He didn't even know her name. The next day she was blowing up his phone, acting like she was his girlfriend. Mo tried to let her down easy, but she wouldn't stop. He finally texted her that he would never be her boyfriend because he doesn't date crazy bitches and that he regretted hooking up with her in the first place. A week later, he heard the news.

Mo almost said her name because that was the worst thing he'd ever done to someone, but he knew it couldn't be her.

"I would've said Mo," Brian admitted.

Mo was jarred from his thoughts at the mention of his name.

"It has to be someone we all have in common," Cora said.

"I used to mess with lots of kids when I was younger," Troy called out.

"You still do," Allie replied.

"So do you. I see you bullying chicks online."

Allie rolled her eyes. "Whatever."

"Come on, guys. Think," Cora said.

Mo thought about middle school and his best friend, Glen Schneider. Even though the mysterious voice was digitized, something in the way it spoke reminded Mo of Glen. Was it word choice or an expression? Mo couldn't put his finger on it exactly. Recently, Glen had DM-ed Mo out the blue. Mo hadn't returned Glen's message. They hadn't talked in five years.

When they went to high school, they had drifted apart. Mo had started to hang with other black kids, and Glen had hung around with other white kids. Mo felt a pang of regret deep in his gut. *Was that really how it went?* Mo thought back to the summer before their freshman year of high school. Mo had spent much of the summer training with the freshman football team, making new friends, and ignoring Glen's texts. Mo and Glen had been best friends through elementary and middle school, but Mo had sensed that he was losing popularity points by associating with Glen. Mo had been too much of a coward to tell Glen to his face how he felt.

As a freshman, Mo was just another scared, skinny kid. He hadn't blossomed into a football star yet. On his first day of high school his freshman year, Mo had looked around the chaotic lunchroom, not sure where to sit. A few older black kids from the football team waved him over to a corner table, and he was grateful to have a place to sit.

Glen had exited the lunch line, holding his lunch tray. Glen had spotted Mo and sauntered over with a big smile.

Mo had looked away, hoping Glen would get the hint.

Glen had sat next to Mo and had said, "Man, I'm glad I found you. It's crowded in here."

The lead kid at the table had said, "What the fuck are you doin', white boy?"

Glen had bowed his head. "Eating lunch?"

"Not here you ain't."

Glen's face had been beet red. "I'm friends with Mo."

"For real?" The lead kid had locked eyes with Mo. "This your boy, Mo?"

Mo hadn't looked at Glen as he shook his head.

"You need to get up on outta here, white boy."

Glen didn't leave though. He had looked at Mo, his brow furrowed. "What are you talking about? You've slept over at my house like a hundred times."

Mo had cringed.

The whole table, except for Glen and Mo, had burst into laughter.

When the laughter subsided, the lead kid had lifted his chin to Mo. "Hey, little man. You a faggot?"

Mo had blushed. "*No.*"

The lead kid had then lifted his chin to Glen, his focus still on Mo. "This punk-ass motherfucker's sayin' you're a faggot. Sleepin' over at his house and shit."

Glen had said, "That's not what I'm saying—"

"Shut the fuck up."

Glen had shut his mouth.

"If I was you, I wouldn't let that motherfucker talk about you like that. You gotta set that bitch ass straight."

Mo had turned to Glen and had said, "Get the fuck outta here, punk-ass bitch."

Glen had opened his mouth to speak, but instead tears had welled in his eyes.

Another kid at the table had said, "This bitch is crying."

The entire table had laughed again. Even Mo had forced a laugh for show.

The lead kid threw a french fry with a little ketchup on the end, smacking Glen in the chest, staining his white T-shirt. By the time Glen had left, tears rolled down his cheeks, and his shirt had a half-dozen stains from ketchup-laden fries.

Mo sucked in a breath and said, "It's Glen Schneider."

Allie and Troy stopped arguing over who was the bigger bully.

Brian winced and said, "Glen Schneider. I beat him up two years ago. He was peeping in my girlfriend's window."

Mo pointed at Troy. "*You* used to bully him."

Troy shrugged. "Never heard of him."

"You called him Babyface."

Troy's eyes widened in recognition. "Babyface McFaggot? Holy shit. I forgot all about that kid."

Mo frowned. "He didn't forget about you."

"Fuck," Allie said to Cora. "We put up those cringy videos of him on Instagram."

Cora tilted her head. "*We?* You did that."

Troy cackled. "I remember those videos. Fucking hilarious."

"It was your idea," Allie said to Cora.

"No, it wasn't," Cora replied. "It was just a hypothetical idea. I told you not to do it."

Allie put her hands on her hips. "He was in love with me. Fucking poems in my locker. Flowers on my car. Always drooling over me. It was disgusting. I had to do *something*. As if I'd give him the time of day."

Mo remembered the videos too. Allie had pretended to be interested in Glen, recording every minute of their fake relationship. Glen's cringey declarations of love made for particularly popular videos, in addition to Glen performing a variety of chores for Allie, ranging from the mundane to the humiliating. The videos went viral, launching Allie's career as an Instagram influencer. Glen had been a pariah, universally mocked and shunned at school. As smart as he was, he didn't know shit about girls.

Cora shook her head. "You didn't have to humiliate him."

"You're such a hypocrite. You were making fun of him in the comments. You think he didn't see that? You had the most liked comments."

Cora blanched.

"We've all done things to him," Mo said.

"Does anyone know if he's good with computers?" Brian asked.

"Glen's smart," Mo replied. "*Especially* with computers. His parents were rich too."

"Were?"

Mo exhaled a heavy breath. "They died in a car accident last year."

Brian grimaced. "Shit. I didn't know that."

"Neither did I," Cora added.

The digitized voice said, "It sounds like all of you deserve to die."

"We know it's you, Glen," Mo said to the ceiling. "I'm sorry for blowing you off freshman year. I was just trying to fit in. I was an asshole."

"I don't know what you're talking about," the voice replied in a clipped but digitized tone.

"I thought about calling you when your parents died. I'm sorry I didn't. I wasn't sure if you wanted to hear from me."

No reply came.

Mo held out his hands in surrender. "Come on, Glen. You don't have to do this. You can let us go. We won't tell anyone, and we'll leave your money."

Still no reply.

# Chapter 16: Cora and The Fort

"Now what?" Allie asked.

"We need to make a plan," Mo replied.

"He's probably watching and listening to us," Brian said.

"You're right. Let's huddle up."

Cora, Allie, Mo, and Brian moved closer, huddling in the middle of the room. Troy stayed near his stash, by the east bookshelf.

"He'll kill one of us by sunrise," Mo whispered.

"He can just shoot at us from above anytime he wants," Brian whispered.

"What if we built a fort out of the books and furniture?" Cora whispered. "We could use the carpet as a roof. We could secure it with the books. Then, we could hide under it, and he wouldn't be able to shoot us from the ceiling."

Mo nodded. "That's a good idea. That would force him to come down here. If that happens, we have a chance."

Allie fidgeted, shifting her weight back and forth from her left foot to her right foot and back again. "A bullet can go through carpet."

"I was thinking we could pile books on top," Cora whispered.

Allie frowned. "Bullets can go through paper too."

"Maybe not," Brian whispered. "I saw this YouTube video where these guys were shooting these books. They called them Yellow Pages. The books were thick, but they did stop the bullets."

"It's better than nothing," Mo whispered.

Allie still fidgeted.

Cora surveyed the room. Books littered the floor. In addition to the television Mo had ripped from the wall, two end tables and a floor lamp were turned over. "Let's start by organizing this mess."

"I have to pee," Allie said.

"No bathroom," Brian replied.

Allie scowled at Brian. "No shit."

Cora pointed at the exposed stone where she and Mo had created a hole in the drywall and had removed the insulation. "That's the best place to pee. Hopefully, it'll filter down to the basement."

Allie looked at the hole, her face puckered. "I'm supposed to put my bare ass in there and pee in front of everyone?"

"I can stand in front of you. We can make everyone turn around."

Allie blew out a breath. "Whatever." She stalked to the west wall and peered into the hole.

Cora grabbed her suit jacket and followed her.

"Everyone, turn around," Allie said.

Mo and Brian faced Troy at the east wall.

"You too, Troy."

Troy smirked. "Nothing I haven't seen before."

"Fuck you."

Cora stood in front of Allie, holding out her suit jacket as a shield.

Allie removed her pantyhose and tossed them on the floor. Then, she pulled her underwear down to midthigh, hiked her skirt, and squatted into the hole on the wall.

Cora turned her head. Allie whizzed, the flow of urine strong, the ammonia smell powerful.

Allie pulled up her underwear and stood. "That's it."

"I can smell your piss from here," Troy called out.

"You sure that's not from pissing your pants?"

Brian faced Allie. "Are you dehydrated? That can cause a strong urine smell."

Allie glared. "Shut up, Brian."

Brian dipped his head and said in a barely audible tone, "I was just trying to help."

The ammonia smell dissipated.

"I have to go too," Mo said, taking his turn at the makeshift urinal.

After bathroom breaks, they stacked the books and straightened up the room. Except for Troy, who sat on a leather chair, guarding his loot.

They put the other leather chairs close together in a line, two by two, the chairs facing outward. Troy refused to donate his chair to the cause. Next, they draped the large oriental rug over the chairs, using the extra slack from the carpet to conceal the sides and to fold in at the seat of the chairs. Then, they piled stacks of heavy hardback books in the chair seats to hold the carpet in place. Finally, they covered the carpet roof with books, roughly the thickness of two long novels, to protect them from bullets.

Cora knelt and looked inside the fort. The living area underneath was only about three feet tall, eight feet long, and four feet wide, although additional legroom was achieved if you slipped your legs under a leather chair. The others stood behind Cora, also checking out the fort.

"Looks small," Brian said.

"We'll fit," Cora said, crawling into the fort. She lay on her back at the far end, slipping her legs under a chair. "Try it out."

Allie climbed inside and lay next to Cora, their bodies touching. Then, Mo crawled inside, contorting his long legs, then squeezing them underneath a leather chair.

Brian was last to crawl inside. "I have to be near the end. I'm claustrophobic." Brian lay next to Mo, his face turned to the opening.

They were jam-packed, their shoulders touching.

"It's gonna be a long night," Mo said.

Troy stuck his head into the fort. "Got room for me?"

"No," everyone said in unison.

Troy scowled. "I see how it is."

Brian sat up straight. "What do you expect? You're a rapist."

"Fuck you guys. I hope Babyface McFaggot kills all of you."

# Chapter 17: Mo and Lights Out

Mo lay on his back in the fort, his legs pinned under a leather chair. His suit jacket was balled up under his head, repurposed as a pillow. The four of them—Cora, Allie, Mo, and Brian—lay tightly together. The overhead light filtered into the fort from the entrance and exit. Mo swallowed. His mouth and throat were dry. Troy was somewhere outside of the fort. The last place Mo saw him was sitting on a leather chair along the east wall, guarding his cash.

Mo glanced at his watch—*11:02 p.m.* He and the others had been in the library of the mansion for thirteen hours, without a drop to drink or anything to eat. Most of that time, they'd been crammed in their makeshift fort.

Allie turned on her side, kneeing Mo in the thigh, and groaning from the effort. "I'm so thirsty."

"We all are," Mo replied, not feeling any pain from Allie's knee.

Allie licked her dry lips. "We need water. I'm seriously going to die of thirst."

"I think that takes three days," Brian said, still near the fort entrance.

Allie sighed. "How long are we gonna stay in here?"

"Until someone finds us or Glen comes down here," Mo replied.

"You really think it's him?" Cora asked.

"Yeah. I do."

"At some point we'll have to pee again," Allie said.

"Or shit," Brian said, flat on his back.

"Gross. Please tell me you don't have to take a dump."

"No, but I do have to piss."

"You go out there, it's a risk," Mo said.

Brian swallowed hard. "He won't kill anyone until sunrise, right?"

"I don't know what he's gonna do."

"Did anyone actually drive here? Or did you guys use the car service?" Cora asked.

"Car service," Mo said.

"Me too," Brian said.

"I used the car service too," Allie said.

"Shit," Mo said.

Cora turned on her side to face the group, her body tight to Allie. "Nobody knows where we are."

"People will notice we're gone, and they'll start looking."

"But when?"

"My parents won't notice for at least a few days," Allie said.

"My mom will notice by tomorrow around lunch," Cora said, "but I doubt she'll do anything."

"My dad might notice tomorrow afternoon when he comes home," Mo said.

"My room's in the basement. I sometimes go days without seeing my parents. They both work long hours," Brian said.

"By tomorrow afternoon, I'm sure someone will come looking for us," Mo said. "We just need to be patient."

"But, how long will it take to find us, *after* they start looking?" Cora asked.

"Maybe they could track our phones," Mo said.

"The ones being jammed?" Brian asked. "I doubt it."

"We're so fucked," Allie said.

Mo took a deep cleansing breath. "We can't give up. All we have to do is stay alive. Someone will eventually find us."

The lights flicked off, the fort descending into total darkness.

Allie squealed, causing Cora and Brian to scream.

"What the hell?" Troy called out from across the room.

"Is everyone okay?" Mo asked.

"I'm okay," Allie replied, her breathing elevated.

"I can't see my hand in front of my face, but I'm okay," Cora said.

"I don't like the dark," Brian said, his voice trembling. "It triggers my claustrophobia."

Mo tapped his phone, the blue screen providing some needed light.

"That's better." Brian grabbed his own phone, the Flashlight app making Mo's blue light superfluous.

Mo turned off his phone, not wanting to deplete the battery. "We should try to get some sleep."

"I still have to piss," Brian said. "I'll be right back."

"This is a bad idea, Brian," Mo said.

"I'm not gonna piss my pants."

"Better than dying."

Brian left the fort, his phone's Flashlight app guiding his way. He peed in the hole in the wall, like they'd all done. He stepped back toward the fort, his footsteps audible.

A gunshot cracked, making everyone shriek, including Troy. Brian ran into the fort and dove, landing on Mo's thighs. His phone landed with the flashlight faceup in the fort. Brian nearly hyperventilated, checking his body for holes. Troy dove into the fort too, partially on top of Brian.

Mo contorted his body away from the guys, crowding Allie and Cora.

Brian and Troy started to wrestle, each accidentally kneeing and elbowing Mo, jostling the heavy leather chairs, their heads hitting the Oriental rug roof.

"Get the hell off me," Brian said, grunting.

"Let me in!" Troy shouted. "I'm a sitting duck out there."

"Stop it!" Mo shouted, sitting up, and pushing the scrum toward the fort entrance. "Calm down."

Brian and Troy stopped grappling, both of them breathing heavily. Brian sat on his haunches inside the fort, next to Mo, whereas Troy sat on his butt, part of his body outside the fort. Troy gave Brian a final shove, knocking him into Mo, and creating space inside the fort. Troy scooted into the vacant space so he was no longer exposed.

"You can't expect me to sit out there alone," Troy said.

"There's not enough room," Mo said.

"Bullshit. We just made enough room."

Mo let out a breath. "It's up to everyone else."

"I don't care. As long as he's not next to me," Allie said.

"I'm not sleeping next to a rapist," Cora said.

"I wouldn't touch you if you paid me, Fivehead," Troy replied.

"I don't want him in here," Brian said, his jaw clenched.

"You need to leave," Mo said to Troy.

"I'm not going anywhere," Troy said. "And, if you force me out, I'll wreck this fucking fort, and we'll all be exposed.

Mo ran his hand over his face, knowing that Troy had won. "Don't *touch* anyone."

"I have to stay on the end," Brian said.

They smushed together tighter, with Cora at the far end, then Allie, Mo, Troy, and Brian at the other end. After some arguing and jockeying for space, everyone eventually settled down.

Mo lay on his back, his eyelids heavy. It took several hours, but Mo's adrenaline dissipated, and he slipped into a deep sleep.

# Chapter 18: Cora and The Game of Life

Grunting and groaning woke Cora from her slumber. She sat up and blinked, trying to adjust to the darkness, but it was pitch-black. "What's happening?" Cora asked, her voice raspy and her throat dry.

Choking came from the opposite end of the fort.

Allie stirred next to Cora. "Are they fighting again?"

Cora groped for her purse, stashed under the chair by her head. She unzipped it and grabbed her phone. She pressed the button on the side and swiped right, waking her phone, and illuminating the fort with a dim blue light. Troy held a knife, straddling Brian, who held his own neck, choking, blood covering his hands.

"Oh, my God! Get off him!" Cora shouted.

Mo sat up, wiping his eyes, his head touching the carpet roof.

Cora pointed a shaky finger at Troy. "He stabbed Brian!"

Troy exited the fort.

Mo locked eyes with Brian and inhaled a sharp breath.

Allie screamed and scrambled over Cora, exiting the fort on the opposite side from Troy.

Brian was on his back, clutching his neck, gagging. Blood spurted from his neck in pulses, dousing his hands in blood and staining his white T-shirt.

"Holy shit." Mo glanced back at Cora.

Cora was speechless, her mouth agape.

Mo grabbed his white button-down shirt from under a chair. He crawled to Brian and pressed the white cotton to Brian's neck, Mo's shirt turning crimson.

Brian convulsed like he was having a seizure. Then it stopped, and Brian's head lolled to the side, his eyes still wide open.

Mo let go of Brian's neck and sat back on his haunches. "*Fuck.*" Mo turned and looked at Cora, who hugged herself, staring at the pool of blood on the floor around Brian's head.

"Did Troy do this?" Mo asked.

"I think so," Cora replied.

Mo crawled over Brian's body and exited the tent. Cora left the tent from the opposite side, so she didn't have to touch Brian.

Troy stood along the east wall bookshelf with his pile of cash, his phone flashlight illuminating his face like a ghoul, and his white T-shirt dotted with blood.

Cora found Allie across the room from Troy. They hugged, both still eyeing Troy.

Mo stalked toward Troy, his fists clenched. "You killed Brian."

Troy held out his bloody knife, his legs wide and defensive. "He attacked me while I was sleeping. Took my knife from my pocket and tried to stab me."

"Bullshit. He was on his back."

"Yeah, because I put him there."

Mo narrowed his eyes. "I don't believe you."

"Ask Cora. She saw."

Cora and Allie walked closer to Mo and Troy, sticking close together.

"All I saw was Troy on top of Brian with the knife," Cora said.

"Allie?" Mo asked. "Did you see anything?"

Allie shook her head. "No."

Mo pivoted back to Troy. "You need to give me that knife."

Troy jabbed the knife at the space between them. "If you come near me, I'll kill you too."

The overhead lights flicked on.

Cora, Allie, and Mo rushed back into the fort. Cora dove over Brian's body landing on top of Allie. Mo dove into the fort from the opposite side, smashing against Allie.

"Ow!" Allie said.

"Sorry," Mo replied.

The digitized voice from above clapped and said, "Good job, Troy. I knew you had it in you. The rest of you cowards can relax. You have another twenty-four hours before I need another death," the voice said.

Mo checked his watch. "It's 5:06. Almost sunrise."

Cora glanced at Brian, his face pale and still. "I can't be in here with him."

"Me neither," Allie said, her face and body turned away from the dead body.

Cora, Mo, and Allie all exited the fort.

"The cowards emerge from their hiding spot," the voice said.

Mo glared at the ceiling. "Why don't you come down here and call me a coward to my face, Glen?"

"I'm not your enemy. Allie, Cora, and Troy are standing between you and freedom and two million dollars. I think you need to get your head in the game."

"Let us go," Cora said. "This isn't a game. Brian's dead."

The digitized voice chuckled. "Life's just one big game, filled with trillions of little games that are played every day. You're either winning or losing. Are you a winner or a loser, Cora?"

Cora opened her mouth to speak but remained silent.

"That's what I thought. This is your chance to change all that. You have a 25 percent chance of walking out of here with two million dollars in cash."

"The cops will find us," Mo said.

The voice chuckled again. "I don't think anyone will ever find you. And whoever wins this game will take their cash and never tell a soul. After all, you can't win without committing at least one murder."

"Nobody's killing anyone anymore," Mo said through gritted teeth. "If you wanna kill us, you'll have to do it yourself."

"I'm sure you're wrong about that."

"I can't believe this is happening," Allie said, huddling with Cora.

"We'll get through this," Cora said.

The mail slot opened, and a single bullet fell from the ceiling. It bounced on the hardwood and rolled toward Cora and Allie. Cora picked it up.

Mo rushed toward her, his hand outstretched. He whispered so Troy couldn't hear, "I still have the gun."

Cora handed the bullet to Mo, who hurried into the fort. Mo returned shortly thereafter and stalked to Troy.

Troy smirked. "Looking for something?" The revolver was on the bookshelf behind Troy, sitting atop his money.

"Give me the gun," Mo said, holding out his hand.

"Give me the bullet," Troy replied.

"You already have a knife."

"Sounds like a *you* problem."

Mo stared at Troy for a long beat. "If you try to stab me or anyone else, I'll kill you."

Troy glared back. "We'll see about that."

"Is it getting hot in here?" Allie asked, removing her blouse, revealing a white tank top. "We need water."

"And food," Troy said.

Allie gave him a *how can you think about eating with a dead body in the room* look.

"I think Glen turned on the heat," Cora said. "We have to find the vents and block them."

Everyone except Troy searched the room, but the vents were on the ceiling.

"*Shit*," Cora said, looking at the vents. "We can't cover them. We can't even reach them."

"I can't stay here in the heat with a dead body," Allie said.

"You mean, *Brian?*" Mo asked, his eyebrows arched. "He was a person."

"Don't act all high and mighty. You hated him."

"Doesn't mean he wasn't a person."

Allie crossed her arms over her chest. "Whatever. We need to at least get him out of the fort."

"Allie's right," Cora said. "With this heat, he'll start to smell soon."

"Where should we put him?" Mo asked.

"Put him by the door," Allie said, stepping back. "I can't touch him."

"When did *we* become *me?*" Mo addressed Troy, not waiting for Allie's response. "You drag him over there. *You* killed him."

"Not happening." Troy still guarded his cash and weapons.

Mo blew out a breath.

"I can help," Cora said.

Mo shook his head. "It'll be easier with one person." Mo went into the fort and dragged Brian out by his feet, leaving a trail of blood across the hardwood.

Allie stared at the blood, her face scrunched up as if she'd eaten a lemon. Then, she looked away.

An envelope dropped from the ceiling, near Troy's feet. Troy grabbed the envelope and opened it.

Cora and Allie tentatively walked over to Troy.

"What is it?" Allie asked.

Troy glanced at the letter, then slipped it into his pocket, and dropped the envelope on the floor. The envelope had TROY written in block letters on the front. "None of your business."

"What are you talking about? It's everyone's business," Allie said.

Mo left Brian near the library door, then returned to the group.

"Glen just dropped a letter to Troy," Cora said, "but he won't tell us what it said."

Mo lifted his chin to Troy. "What did it say?"

"That's my business," Troy replied. "It had my name on it."

"We should go back to the fort," Mo said, addressing Cora and Allie. "It's not safe out here."

Allie frowned. "It wasn't safe for Brian in the fort."

"I'm not going back in there with Troy," Cora said. "He still has that knife."

"And now he has a gun," Allie added.

"I was defending myself, and the gun has no bullets," Troy replied.

"I agree with Allie and Cora," Mo said, turning to Troy. "You can't be in the fort, especially since you're hiding that letter from us."

Troy slipped the revolver in his pocket. "Fuck it. I don't give a shit. If you think some fucking books will protect you, you're out of your mind."

# Chapter 19: Mo and Fiji Water

Mo was in the fort with Allie and Cora. They had been hiding in there for the last four hours, the temperature slowly but surely rising. They were all soaked with sweat. Cora fanned herself with her hand. Allie took off her skirt and tank top, revealing white lacy underwear.

Allie glared at Mo. "Keep your eyes and hands to yourself."

"Don't flatter yourself." Mo removed his dress pants and white T-shirt, revealing his boxer briefs, and feeling immediate relief from the heat.

Cora gasped at the burns on his chest. "What happened to you?"

Mo scowled.

"Sorry. That was rude."

"Don't worry about it." Mo lay on his back, staring at the Oriental rug roof.

Cora removed her skirt and undershirt too, revealing white cotton underwear and a light blue bra.

A heavy *thump* came from outside the fort.

"What was that?" Allie asked, sitting up.

Then another heavy *thump* came, followed by six more in quick succession.

Mo peeked out of the fort, as Troy picked up two water bottles from the floor. "It's water," Mo said.

"Oh, my God. I'm literally dying of thirst," Allie said.

"Me too," Cora said.

"I'll get the water," Mo said, as he crawled out of the fort.

Troy sat on his leather chair, his back to the bookshelf and his neatly stacked two million dollars. He guzzled a sixteen-ounce water, an empty bottle next to him. Six full plastic bottles were scattered on the floor.

"There were eight waters. I only took two," Troy said.

Mo narrowed his eyes at Troy, skeptical of his fairness. Mo collected the remaining water bottles from the floor and crawled back into the fort. He left four bottles at the entrance to the fort, crawling inside carrying a Deer Park water in one hand and a Fiji water in the other hand. He set the bottles next to Cora and said, "We each get two. I'll get the rest."

"Give me the Fiji," Allie said.

Cora scowled. "Why do you feel so entitled to everything?"

Mo shook his head, turned around on his knees, and grabbed two more bottles, both Fiji waters.

"Do you really care which water you drink?" Allie asked.

"It's not about the brand of water," Cora replied. "It's that you always have to have everything. You always have to be better than me. I'm sick of it."

"I'm literally dying of thirst," Allie replied. "Just give me a fucking water."

Mo crawled back in, carrying two more Fiji waters.

"Here's your snobby water." Cora tossed the Fiji water at Allie unnecessarily hard.

The water bottle hit Allie in the chest. "Ow! You hit my tit."

"Whatever."

"Come on guys," Mo said, sitting on his butt, his head brushing the roof. "It's too hot to be arguing."

Allie unscrewed the Fiji water bottle and took a long drink.

Mo handed a Fiji water to Cora. "Water's water. I'll drink the Deer Park."

Cora took the water. "Thanks."

Mo opened his Deer Park water and took a drink.

Cora opened her Fiji water.

Allie dropped her water bottle, wheezing for air.

Cora put the bottle of Fiji water to her lips.

Mo smacked the bottle out of Cora's hand, precious water spilling on the hardwood. "Don't drink the water!"

Allie trembled, holding her chest, still wheezing for air.

"Oh, my God. Allie!" Cora said, grabbing her friend by the shoulders. "What's wrong?"

"I think she was poisoned," Mo said.

"What do we do?"

"I don't know."

Troy appeared at the fort entrance, watching the scene.

Allie's face turned blue. Her body jerked uncontrollably. Cora tried to hold her upright, in a sitting position, but the seizure was too strong. Allie slumped to her side, still shaking. The seizure went on for the longest minute of Mo's life.

Then, Allie went limp.

Cora shook her friend, sobbing. "No. No, no, no. Please wake up. Please, Allie. Wake up."

Mo put his hand on Cora's shoulder. "She's gone."

Cora hugged herself and rocked back and forth, still crying.

Troy squatted at the fort entrance. "What the hell happened?"

"I think the water's poisoned," Mo said.

"I drank the water. Nothing happened."

"So did I. I think the poison was only in the Fiji water." Mo picked up a full Fiji bottle and a Deer Park bottle. "Look. No safety cap on the Fiji water. They've been opened. But the Deer Park bottle still has the safety cap." Mo grabbed his half-empty Deer Park water bottle and handed it to Cora. "This is safe. I drank half of it already."

Cora still rocked and cried, ignoring the water.

Mo screwed on the cap and left it next to Cora. Then, he dragged Allie's body to the door, leaving Cora in the fort. He placed Allie next to Brian, who smelled faintly of feces and urine, but it wasn't overwhelming. His body still appeared to be intact, with little noticeable decomposition.

Troy again sat on his leather chair, nursing a half-full bottle of Deer Park water. The corner of his mouth turned up for an instant, but Mo saw it.

Mo stopped in his tracks and stared at Troy for a long moment.

"What?" Troy asked. "This wasn't my fault. I wasn't anywhere near her."

Mo looked at the Deer Park bottle in Troy's grasp. "Why didn't you take any Fiji waters?"

Troy shrugged. "I was thirsty. I took the first two waters I saw."

Mo pursed his lips. "Lucky for you."

"What the fuck are you trying to say?"

"You knew those Fiji waters were poisoned, didn't you?"

"How the fuck would I know?"

Mo lifted his chin. "Lemme see that letter."

"No."

"I know what you did, motherfucker. Stay away from us."

Troy stood from his chair, standing two inches taller than Mo. "Us? It's *us* now?"

Mo nodded. "What are you gonna do about it?"

"You'll regret this."

Mo pointed at Troy. "Touch me or Cora, and you'll be the one with regrets." Mo crawled into the fort.

Cora sat cross-legged, weeping, her chin to her chest. Mo put his arm around her, and she buried her face in his chest, her body heaving with her sobs.

After a time, her crying eased and finally stopped. Cora looked up at Mo and said, "None of us are leaving here alive."

# Chapter 20: Mo and Under the Cover of Darkness

That night, Mo and Cora lay alone in the fort, next to a puddle of Brian's dried blood. The lights were off, making it impossible for Mo to see past the nose on his face. The smell of body odor mixed with ammonia from the nearby makeshift urinal, along with the increasingly fetid smell of feces and decomposition coming from the dead bodies. Mo figured it was true. *You do shit yourself when you die.*

Mo now wore his dress pants and T-shirt, while Cora wore her skirt, undershirt, and blouse again. Glen or whoever was controlling this "game" had turned off the heat. Mo's stomach rumbled.

"You hungry?" Cora whispered.

"Yeah. You?" Mo whispered back.

"More thirsty."

"Me too."

"You think Troy will try to kill us tonight?"

"I don't know."

Cora woke up her phone, bathing them in blue light.

"How much battery you got left?" Mo whispered.

Cora frowned. "Six percent."

"Mine's out. We should save your battery. We might have to make a 9-1-1 call."

Cora turned off her phone. "I know. It's so dark though." She swallowed hard. "I'm scared. What if Troy or Glen comes for us?"

"Don't worry. We'll hear them. Without sight, our other senses are stronger. And, if I get ahold of either of them, they're done."

"You really think it's Glen Schneider?"

"Yeah. I'm almost certain," Mo whispered. "When we were in middle school, we had this Spanish teacher, Ms. Vergara."

"I think I remember her. Didn't she quit?" Cora whispered back.

"She was fired. Glen had something to do with that. So did I."

"Whoa. What happened?"

"Glen always got straight As, except in Spanish. Ms. Vergara embarrassed him, constantly making fun of his accent. He was already shy about talking in class. I wasn't doing too well in Spanish either. She told me I spoke Spanish like a black beast."

Cora sucked in a breath. "That's racist. Is that why they fired her?"

"No. I never said anything about that. I didn't really understand that she was being racist, but I understood her tone and the expression on her face. Glen wanted to get back at her, and so did I, so we found out where she lived and we rode our bikes there. It was only a few miles away. It was a Saturday night, and I was spending the night at Glen's. His parents were gone a lot."

"You guys were really good friends, huh?"

Mo nodded to himself in the dark. "Best friends." Mo took a deep breath. "It was just after dark. We hid our bikes in the woods across the street and snuck up to her house. We knocked on her door. Then we ran back to the woods. It was anticlimactic. She came out, looked around, and went back inside. The weird thing was that she looked pretty. I expected to see her in some sweats, but she wore a nice dress with heels. She looked a lot better than she did at school. Glen wanted to put a flaming bag of dog shit on her front porch. Of course, we didn't have dog shit or a lighter or even a bag. I wanted to get some toilet paper and throw it in her trees." Mo thought about Glen's face that night, half lit by the moonlight, too serious for a prank.

"What happened? Did you get the toilet paper?"

"No. Before we had a chance to do anything, a car pulled into her driveway, and a guy got out, carrying flowers. A Jefferson Middle School bumper sticker was on the car. The garage light was on, so we had a good view of the guy, and we were shocked. It was Principal Carlson."

"Wow. Principal Carlson?" Cora whispered, trying to contain her excitement.

"Yeah. So, Carlson went to the front door, and Ms. Vergara answered the door, before he even knocked. He gave her the flowers. They kissed on the front porch. Then they went in the house. We knew Principal Carlson was married. He had pictures of his family on his desk. I had been in his office enough times to notice them. I said something to Glen like, 'I think Principal Carlson's having an affair.' Glen said he wanted to get pictures. I was like, 'What? How do we do that?' But he didn't answer. Glen was already running for the house, so I ran after him."

"Did he get pictures?"

"Yeah. He did. We looked in Ms. Vergara's bedroom window, and they were undressing. Then they were having sex. I told Glen we should leave, but he wouldn't, and he took a bunch of pictures with his phone."

"*Eww*. Gross."

Mo blew out a breath. "That wasn't even the worst part. Glen sent anonymous copies to Principal Carlson, with a note that said, if he didn't fire Ms. Vergara, the pictures would be sent to Carlson's wife. Next thing we knew, Vergara was gone."

"Wow. That's some serious shit," Cora whispered. "How old were you guys?"

"It was eighth grade. I think we were thirteen at the time. That's when I knew Glen wasn't quite right."

The floor groaned near the fort.

"Did you hear that?" Cora whispered.

"Yeah." Mo sat up.

Cora grabbed her phone and tried to turn it on, but it was out of charge. "Shit. Mine's out now."

A crash came from just outside the fort. It sounded like stacks of books hitting the wood floor.

"It's Troy," Mo said. "He's destroying the fort. I'll be back." Mo crawled out of the entrance.

Cora said, "It could be a trap."

Mo didn't listen. The room was dimly lit from the blue glow of Troy's phone, sitting faceup on the roof of the fort. No doubt his expensive phone had a long-lasting battery. Troy removed books from the roof of the fort by the stack, dumping them on the floor.

"What the fuck are you doing?" Mo said, approaching Troy with his fists clenched.

"What's it look like I'm doing?" Troy replied, not stopping with his demolition. "Come sunrise, I won't be the only one out in the open."

Cora exited the fort. "Stop it, Troy!"

Troy stopped and smirked at Cora, his hand on a stack of books. Like a mischievous cat, he pushed the stack of books off the fort, sending them crashing to the floor.

Mo shoved Troy to the ground.

The digitized voice from above said, "Troy knew the Fiji water was poisoned."

"I knew it. You killed Brian *and* Allie," Mo said, standing over Troy.

"You're sick," Cora said.

Heavy metal music pumped from the ceiling speakers, a furious drumbeat and a haunting bass guitar in the background. The music was so loud that Mo couldn't hear anything else. Troy rose to his feet, extracted his knife from his pocket, and opened the blade. That's when

Troy's phone went black, the blue screen vanquished to save energy.

Mo moved to his right through the total darkness, not wanting to be in the same place, lightly stepping on and around books as he went. Mo kept stepping to his right until he felt the wall. Then, he crept along the wall until he was in the corner. Here, he crouched and touched the floor, hoping to feel someone's approach through reverberations in the hardwood.

The overhead light flicked on for an instant. In that brief time, Mo didn't see Troy or Cora, but Troy might've seen Mo. Just in case, he crept along the wall, headed for the southwest corner. Midway there, the overhead light flicked on again, this time for a few seconds. Troy stalked along the north wall. He spotted Mo and rushed toward him, his blade in hand. Mo froze, like a deer in headlights. Troy tripped on a book, falling to one knee. This broke Mo from his fog, and he rushed to meet Troy, who had righted himself and now braced for the collision.

The lights went out again, but it was too late for Mo to stop his attack. Mo crashed into Troy in the pitch dark. Mo groped for Troy's wrists, trying to gain control of the pocketknife. Troy brought his right hand down like a hammer, plunging the knife deep into Mo's thigh. Mo reflexively grabbed Troy's forearm and wrist, twisting his wrist until it cracked, and Troy screamed, letting go of the knife.

Troy's cries of agony were barely audible over the music. Mo extracted the knife from his thigh, without a whimper or even a grunt. He stabbed wildly in the dark, first connecting with soft flesh, then hard bone, unsure of exactly what part of Troy's body Mo was hitting. He stabbed and stabbed, manic, Troy's body used like a pin cushion. Blood spattered on Mo's face and chest. Troy collapsed to the floor. Mo fell atop his former teammate, still stabbing, but Troy was silent now.

The light flicked back on, and the music stopped.

Cora screamed.

# Chapter 21: Cora's Best Shot

Cora's scream echoed through the library. Mo straddled Troy, staring at Troy's lifeless, bloody body. In a daze, Mo shut the pocketknife and shoved it into his pocket. He slid off Troy, Mo's left leg stiff. Mo sat on the floor, his legs straight out in front of him. He gripped his left thigh, blood staining his slacks and oozing between his fingers.

Cora rushed to Mo, kneeling at his side. "Oh, my God. He stabbed you."

Mo nodded, no sign of pain on his face. "I need a tourniquet."

"A what?"

"We have to cut the blood flow. Otherwise I'll bleed to death."

Cora's stomach tumbled. She swallowed the hot bile creeping up her throat. Her sister appeared in her mind. Floating in the bathtub, pale skin, red water.

"*Cora*. I need your help," Mo said, urgency in his voice.

Cora blinked, returning to reality, her vision blurry through her tears. "I don't know how to help."

"I do. Go get my keys and my tie. They're inside my shoes in the fort, under one of the chairs."

Cora hurried to the fort, crawling inside, concentrating on the task, and suppressing her subconscious thoughts. She searched under the leather chairs, finding Mo's dress shoes. She found his necktie and a single key attached to a key ring, then attached to a large carabiner.

Cora rushed back to Mo's side, holding up the key ring and tie. "What now?"

"Untie that Windsor knot, then set everything in my lap," Mo said.

Cora nodded and did as instructed.

"Apply pressure to my leg, right where my hands are."

Cora placed her hands on Mo's.

"I'm gonna remove my hands, so I can work on this tourniquet. Hold pressure on my wound to limit the bleeding. Understand?"

Cora nodded. "I think so."

Sweat beaded on Mo's forehead. "On three. One, two, three." Mo removed his hands, and Cora pressed on his wound, her fingers slickening with blood.

Cora expected him to cry out, but he didn't even grunt.

Mo moved decisively, as if he'd practiced. He wrapped the tie around his thigh, above his wound. He slipped one end of the tie through the key ring, and tied his tie into a loose knot. He added the carabiner to the knot, then tightened the knot. He turned the carabiner a few times, tightening the tourniquet. Finally, he clamped the carabiner to the key ring, holding the tourniquet in place.

"Is that it?" Cora asked.

Mo nodded and exhaled. "You can let go."

Cora let go of Mo's leg, expecting blood to flow, but the blood stopped. "How did you know how to do that?"

Mo didn't answer for several seconds, as if savoring a memory. He looked ashen but relaxed. "My mom. She used to worry about me a lot."

Cora glanced at his thigh. "Does it hurt?"

Mo shook his head and lay back on the hardwood.

"You must have a high pain tolerance."

"You could say that."

"We have to get you to the hospital."

"I don't think I'm gonna make it," Mo said.

Cora swallowed the lump in her throat. "Don't say that."

Clapping came from the speakers above them. "Very good, Mo. I was hoping it would be you and Cora in the end."

Cora stood and peered up at the ceiling. "He'll die if we don't get him to a hospital."

"That's not how this game works," the digitized voice replied. "Winner takes all, and the winner *must* kill someone. There are four ways this game can end. Mo can kill Cora, and he wins the game. Cora can kill Mo, and she wins the game. If Mo dies from his wounds, Cora can only win if she kills herself, in which case I'll send the money to her family. If she doesn't kill herself, I'll be forced to kill Cora, and nobody wins. Nobody's getting out of here without blood on their hands."

"We're done with your games." Cora knelt next to Mo and held his hand.

Mo said, "I'm cold."

"Hold on." Cora went to the fort, grabbed her suit jacket along with Mo's, and returned. She knelt next to Mo again and covered his upper body with his jacket. Then, she placed her jacket under his head as a makeshift pillow. "Is that better?"

"Yeah."

Cora sat next to him and took his hand again. "I don't know what to do."

Mo shut his eyes for a few seconds.

Cora wasn't sure if he'd open them again.

When he did, he motioned with his finger to come closer.

Cora leaned close to him.

He reached into his pocket; then he took her hand, the bullet wedged between their palms. He whispered in her ear, "Get the gun from Troy. It's probably in his pocket or with the money. I want you to shoot me. It's the only way."

Cora stiffened and spoke in a hushed whisper. "Absolutely not. We can save the bullet for that asshole upstairs."

Mo took a ragged breath. "He won't come down here until that bullet is used."

"I won't shoot you."

"Get the gun. Either way … you'll need it."

Cora went to Troy's bloody body. He was on his back, his T-shirt soaked with blood, his face pale, and his eyes wide open. She patted the pockets of his pants, feeling the hard imprint of the metal revolver. She extracted the gun from his pocket and went back to Mo, kneeling at his side. "Okay. I got it."

"You know how to load it?"

"No."

Mo held out his hands. "Here."

Cora gave the gun and bullet to Mo. He opened the cylinder, inserted the single bullet, lined up the cylinder to fire the bullet on the next trigger pull, and closed the cylinder. Mo returned the gun to Cora and whispered, "There's no safety, so keep your finger off the trigger, until you're ready to fire. Just line up the sights and pull the trigger."

Her hands trembled as she took the revolver. "Did your mom teach you how to shoot too?"

Mo forced a smile. "Glen's dad did. Took us to the range a few times. Glen was always into guns."

Cora grimaced and set the revolver on the floor next to her.

A single sheet of paper floated from the ceiling, landing several feet away from them. Cora let go of Mo's hand, walked to the page, and picked it up. She read the text string, dated the day after her sister's suicide.

"What is it?" Mo asked.

Cora ignored Mo, her undivided attention on the words on the page.

**Craig**: Didn't u hook up with Laura Hinton at my party two weeks ago? I saw u two go in the guest bedroom

**Mo**: I didn't know she was fucking crazy.

**Craig**: She was all over u. Not ur fault

**Mo**: Who else knows I was with her?

**Craig**: Idk

**Mo**: Don't tell anyone. They might blame me. This is a fucking nightmare.

**Craig**: Relax man. Just cuz u hit it don't mean her death is ur fault

**Mo**: I was an asshole after. She was blowing up my phone and I told her to fuck off. Said she was a crazy bitch.

"What is it?" Mo asked, still laying on his back.

Cora looked up from the text string and walked over to Mo, standing over him. "Does the name Laura Hinton mean anything to you?

Mo winced, not from the pain in his leg. "I can explain. It was a one-night stand. The girl was all over me. If I knew she was so unstable, I never would have …"

Tears filled Cora's eyes. "Fucked her? Treated her like a slut?"

Mo winced again. "Was she your friend?"

"She was my sister! Had you shown her a fucking ounce of kindness, she'd still be here."

Mo showed his hands. "I'm sorry, Cora. I didn't know."

Cora balled up the paper and threw it at Mo. She grabbed the revolver from the floor, aimed it at Mo, her hand shaky, her finger on the trigger. Tears streamed down her face.

Mo blinked, and a tear slipped from his eye. "It's easy to miss with your hand shaking like that. If you're gonna shoot me, you better put that gun to my chest because you only got one shot. I'd rather it be a quick death."

"Do it, Cora," said the digitized voice from above. "Do it, and this will all be over. You'll leave here unharmed, with two million dollars in cash. All you have to do is pull the trigger."

She let out a primal scream.

Mo braced himself for the gunshot.

Cora lowered the gun to her side and glared at the ceiling. "I won't do it. You'll have to kill me."

"All you have to do is put the gun to his temple and pull the trigger, and all your problems vanish," the voice said.

She looked down at Mo and shook her head. "I won't do it."

"You have to," Mo replied. "If you don't, we'll both die." Mo motioned with his finger again, more tears coming now. "I'll show you where."

Cora knelt next to Mo, her heart pounding.

"Hold on to the gun," Mo said. "You have to be the one who pulls the trigger."

Cora nodded.

Mo guided the revolver in Cora's hand, pressing the barrel to his chest, and the suit jacket. "Hold it right there. With both hands."

Cora put both hands on the grip, holding the revolver steady.

Mo tucked his hands at his sides, back under the jacket. "Pull the trigger."

Cora sobbed. "I can't. I can't."

Mo cried too. "Please, Cora. Do it now."

Cora closed her eyes and pulled the trigger. The gun popped, the noise deafening. The smell of smoke and sulfur filled her nostrils. She opened her eyes. A small hole pierced Mo's suit jacket. Cora lifted his jacket. Blood stained his T-shirt, spreading and mixing with the blood spatter from Troy.

Like Brian, Mo quaked with the death throes, as if his heart had exploded in his chest.

Cora dropped the gun on the floor and stepped back, trembling, and watching him die. The death throes ceased, and he was gone, his head lolled to the side. She wiped tears from her eyes and shouted at the ceiling, "Are you happy now, you fucking creep?"

No response came.

"Let me out!"

Still no response.

A few minutes later, the heavy door creaked open, stopped by the dead bodies, opening just enough for a man to slip through. Cora approached the door tentatively, hoping to go home. A doughy man wearing camouflage fatigues and white sneakers entered the library, stepping over the bodies. He held a military-style rifle, his face covered with a ski mask that resembled a smiling skull.

The man aimed his rifle at Cora.

Cora raised her hands over her head and backed up. "You promised you'd let me go."

The man stepped closer, his dark eyes laser focused.

Cora backpedaled, eventually stopping with her back to the north wall, near the fireplace. "Please. Just let me go. I won't say anything. I *can't* say anything. I killed Mo."

The man laughed. "You had it right when you told Mo that nobody's leaving here alive."

Cora sniffled, sucking back mucus. "I know they hurt you. I understand why you're mad, but this isn't the way to fix it."

The man pulled off his ski mask, revealing his chubby baby face and his identity.

Cora recognized Glen from school and the Instagram videos. *Mo was right.*

Glen sneered at Cora. "*They?* You think you're any better?"

*I've seen his face. He can't let me go now.* "I never did anything to you."

"I saw you encouraging Allie in the Insta comments. You're so weak that you'd rather join in my humiliation than run the risk of being bullied yourself."

"You're right. I'm sorry." Cora still held up her arms. "I *was* afraid of being bullied if I didn't join in. I was wrong. I'm so sorry. Please, Glen. Let me go."

Glen narrowed his eyes. "You're no different."

"I was bullied too. Troy and all his buddies called me Fivehead. They spread that private picture of me."

Glen frowned. "So what? Troy bullied me for years. Did a lot more than call me Babyface McFaggot."

"He was an asshole," Cora replied, trying to build trust.

Glen frowned again and let the rifle hang from the shoulder strap, the barrel still aimed vaguely in Cora's direction, and his hands still on the grips. "Did he pull your pants down in the locker room and shove the end of a shampoo bottle in your ass?"

Cora cringed.

"Brian beat me up for looking at his precious Emily. She was the one who kept looking at me in class. You know all about Allie. I was in love with her, and she humiliated me. And Mo was the worst of the worst. He was my best friend, and he threw me away like trash. He's the reason for all this. Nobody picked on me when he was my friend. As soon as he dropped me, that's when it started."

"I'm so sorry, Glen," Cora said, her hands shaking. "Please let me go. I'll do anything."

"Too late." Glen raised his rifle again.

Cora's eyes bulged at the movement coming from the floor next to Glen.

Mo held the pocketknife, its blade glinting in the artificial light. In one sharp motion, Mo sliced through Glen's sock and his Achilles tendon.

Glen screeched in pain and collapsed to the floor on his side, the rifle now pointed at Mo, who was also on his side facing Glen. Mo dropped the knife and grabbed the barrel of the rifle with two hands, moving it away from his face just as Glen fired, the bullets spraying over Mo's shoulder and ear, and into a bookshelf.

Cora fell to the floor and covered her head. Bullets popped in rapid succession, the noise deafening. Sulfur and the smell of fire hung in the air.

Glen rose to his knees and yanked the rifle from Mo's hands. Then, Glen jabbed Mo in the face with the butt of his rifle, the impact causing blood to squirt from Mo's nostrils. Mo was still on his side, dazed, like a fighter down for the count. Glen raised his rifle, aiming the barrel at Mo.

Cora sprinted from her crouched position. She crashed into the rifle, causing Glen to fire a burst of bullets that went wide right of his target. Glen turned the rifle on Cora. She grabbed the barrel as Mo had, but the barrel scorched her hands, and she let go.

Glen squinted as he aimed the rifle at Cora from his knees.

Cora showed her palms, wincing, waiting for the end.

Mo staggered to his full height, using his good leg. Cora peered over Glen's head at the zombie rising from the dead. Glen pivoted on his knees, turning the gun toward Mo, and firing. At the same time Mo fell forward, plunging the pocketknife into Glen's chest, and falling onto his old friend. Bullets *whizzed* past Mo's head. Glen fell on his back, cushioning Mo's fall.

Glen wheezed, the rifle wedged between the former friends. Glen coughed, and blood came from his mouth. Mo rolled off Glen to his back. Glen groped for the trigger on his rifle. Cora rushed over to Glen and grabbed the rifle from his grasp, the strap catching on the back of Glen's neck. Cora yanked harder, the strap sliding over Glen's dark hair. She set the rifle atop the fort, fairly certain Glen wouldn't be standing anytime soon.

The red handle of the pocketknife protruded from Glen's chest. He choked and coughed, more blood spurting from his mouth. Mo lay next to him, covered in blood, holding his left pectoral, where Cora had shot him.

Cora rushed to Mo's side. "You're alive!"

Mo's face was covered in blood spatter from Glen. Between heavy breaths, he said, "I'm a good ... actor. The gun wasn't ... any internal organs."

Cora was frantic. "What do I do? Do we need another tourniquet?"

Mo shook his head. "Get cotton shirt. ... Call ... ambulance."

Cora removed her cotton blouse, exposing her undershirt. She balled up the blouse and pressed it to Mo's chest wound. Mo put his hand atop hers. "I can ... do it. Call ... ambulance."

"Our phones are dead."

"Check ... Glen's pocket. Always has ... phone."

Glen gasped, his lips and chin smeared with blood, his face turning blue.

Cora expected Glen to grab her, but he didn't move as she searched his pockets, and found his phone in the front pocket of his fatigues. The phone was password protected. "You know his password?"

"Glen the ... great. No spaces."

"Capitalization?"

Mo shook his head, still holding his chest wound.

Cora thumb-typed the password, and Glen's phone came to life. There was no service. "I'll be right back." Cora ran from the room in her bare feet, jumping over the dead bodies, and running down the hall to the front door. She looked at the phone, and there was still no service, so she stepped outside into the night, illumination coming from the lights on the portico and the nearly full moon. *Two bars!*

She dialed 9-1-1.

"Nine-one-one, what is your emergency?"

Cora spoke rapidly. "My friend was stabbed and shot. He's lost a lot of blood. We need an ambulance. I don't know where I am."

"I'm requesting your location. It may take a minute or two. Are you in danger at the moment?"

"No. I'm safe."

"May I have your name please? Your phone is listed to a Glen Schneider, but I presume that's not you."

"I'm Cora Hinton. Glen Schneider trapped us in this room and tried to make us kill each other."

"Is Glen Schneider still on the premises?"

"Yes, but he's badly hurt. He can't move."

"Who else is with you, Cora?"

"Maurice Williams." She swallowed, her throat dry. "Everyone else is dead."

"Do either of them have any weapons?"

"No."

"Do you have any weapons?"

"No."

"We have your location now, Cora. Help is on the way."

Cora turned back to the house. "I have to help Mo. Please hurry." Cora hung up the phone and ran back to the library. She rushed back to Mo's side. Glen lay next to him, no longer breathing, his eyes vacant, and his face blue. Mo lay on his back, his eyes closed, and his hands still applying pressure to his gunshot wound.

Cora knelt and put her hand atop his. "An ambulance is coming."

Mo opened his eyes. "The money."

"What about it?" Cora asked.

"Put it ... my briefcase, ... throw it ... in woods. You can ... come back ... for it."

Cora glanced at the neatly stacked cash on the bookshelf. "I can't do that. It's illegal. Glen's probably recording this anyway."

Mo shook his head. "He wouldn't. He was ... paranoid."

"It's still illegal."

"You ... earned it."

Cora glanced back at the money again. "Only if we split it."

Mo nodded and said, "Hurry."

Cora found Mo's briefcase, leaning against a leather chair. She rushed to the bookshelf, opened the briefcase, and set it on the floor. She stuffed as much cash as she could in the briefcase, her heart beating like a heavy metal drummer. Cora shut and latched the briefcase. "I'll be right back."

Mo nodded again, still holding his chest.

Cora hiked her skirt and ran outside, around the mansion to the backyard. The lush grass was soft on her feet. The dew wet her feet and ankles. She sprinted for the woods, carrying the briefcase. She slowed as she reached the trees, more careful with her barefoot steps. She walked on roots, decomposed leaves, and smooth rocks. The *whoosh* of water was nearby.

After thirty yards into the woods, the forest opened to a fast-moving creek and a starry night. Cora stopped at the edge of the creek bed, with a steep downslope and a drop of about ten feet. The creek was bordered on both sides with smooth stones and moss. She thought about climbing down to the creek bed to find a good place to hide the briefcase, but she heard faint sirens in the distance.

Cora found a downed tree, tight to the cliff edge. She dropped the briefcase between the cliff edge and the tree. Then, she ran toward the house, less careful with her feet. Once in the backyard, the sirens sounded closer. Her legs and lungs burned as she sprinted uphill, toward the house. Her dirty feet were cleansed as she ran through the wet grass. She sprinted around the right side of the house to the front, where she bent over, her hands on her knees, struggling for breath. Red and blue lights came from the long driveway in the distance. The sirens pierced the air. Two police cars and an ambulance parked in front.

Four police officers approached her, guns drawn. "On the ground! On your stomach, your hands held out front. Now!"

Cora lay on her stomach, her hands and legs splayed out like a starfish. Her heart pounded, thinking they'd seen her stash the money somehow. A burly officer cuffed her hands behind her back and helped her to her feet. He frisked her for weapons.

"My friend needs help," Cora said. "He's been shot and stabbed."

Another officer asked, "Where's your friend?"

"Turn left as soon as you get into the house. Go to the library at the end of the hall," Cora said.

Three officers went inside.

"Are you Cora Hinton?" the burly officer asked.

"Yes."

"Are you injured?"

"No."

The burly officer prodded Cora to a cruiser. "Let's go."

Cora walked toward the police car, the officer's hand guiding her. "Why am I in handcuffs? I didn't do anything."

"We don't know that yet. We have to make sure the scene is safe for the paramedics. We have a report of multiple homicides here. Is that true?"

Cora nodded.

The burly officer opened a door to the police car and helped Cora inside. "Watch your head." With Cora in the back seat, the officer asked, "What the hell happened here?"

Cora dipped her head. "It's a long story."

"You'll have to tell us everything."

Cora swallowed hard. The burly officer shut the door.

Cora watched the front door for Mo. One of the police officers ran outside and beckoned the paramedics. Three paramedics exited the ambulance. One went with the officer, carrying a large med kit bag. The other two removed a gurney from the back of the ambulance and wheeled it inside the mansion. Cora envisioned Mo dead on the gurney, his face covered with a sheet.

Several minutes later, the paramedics appeared. Mo was on the gurney, his face uncovered, except for the oxygen mask. Cora wondered how he took that gunshot without even a whimper.

# Chapter 22: Mo's Curse

Mo's hospital bed propped him partially upright. He resembled a mummy, watching television. His left pectoral, left thigh, nose, and hands were all bandaged. The surgeon had removed the .38 caliber bullet from his left pectoral. His broken nose had been reset. His hands were healing from the second-degree burns he had suffered from grabbing the red-hot barrel of Glen's rifle. His thigh had been cleaned and stitched from the stab wound. Nothing actually hurt, but he had to be careful not to impede his healing.

Mo's father, Reggie, sat bedside in a chair, reading a thick biography, glasses perched on the end of his nose.

The local news anchor spoke, with a picture of Glen's parents on the television screen. "Police are now investigating the mysterious car accident from eleven months ago."

Reggie looked up from his book. "Haven't you seen enough of that?"

Mo grabbed the remote from the overbed table and changed the channel to ESPN. He watched baseball highlights for a few minutes, muting the television during the commercial break. Mo addressed his father. "You don't need to be here every day. I'm sure you wanna get back to work."

Reggie looked over his reading glasses. "There's no place I'd rather be."

Mo smiled.

Reggie went back to his book.

A nurse entered the hospital room. She stepped aside, revealing the woman behind her, and said, "Maurice, you have a visitor."

Cora stepped forward with a hardback book in hand.

Reggie met Cora in the middle of the hospital room. He held out his hand and said, "You must be Cora."

"I am." Cora shook his hand, still holding the book with her left.

"I'm Reggie Williams. Mo's father."

"It's so nice to meet you, Mr. Williams," Cora replied.

Reggie's smile widened, and he covered her hand with his. "The pleasure's all mine, young lady." Reggie let go of Cora and said, "I appreciate what you did for my son. He wouldn't be here if it wasn't for you."

Mo waved at Cora from the hospital bed.

"He was the one who saved me," Cora said, her eyes flicking to Mo, then back to Reggie.

"I'm glad you had each other in that house of horrors," Reggie said, using the same moniker that had been used by the press. "I never liked that kid."

"I didn't know him, ... not really anyway."

"I'll let you two talk. I'm headed for the cafeteria, if you want anything."

"No, thank you. I'm fine," Cora replied.

"Son?" Reggie asked, turning to Mo.

"I'm good. Thanks, Dad."

Reggie left the room.

Cora approached the bed, wearing makeup and a sundress. "How are you feeling?"

"Not bad. Considering," Mo replied.

Cora looked at the floor. "I'm sorry I didn't come sooner."

"I understand. After what I did, I wasn't sure ..."

Cora raised her gaze, her eyes narrowed at Mo.

"Your sister, Laura." Mo ran his bandaged hand over his face and exhaled. "I wish I could go back and change it. I'm very sorry, Cora."

Cora pursed her lips. "I wish I could change it too, but it's not your fault. I'd rather not talk about it, if that's okay with you."

"I understand."

Cora handed the book to Mo. "I thought you might like this."

Mo took the book, silently reading the title—*The Agent: My 40-Year Career Making Deals and Changing the Game* by Leigh Steinberg. "This looks good. Thank you." Mo set the book on the overbed table.

"You're welcome."

Mo gestured to the chair next to his bed. "Wanna sit down?"

"Thanks." Cora sat. "I'm assuming you heard about Glen's parents?"

"Yeah. They were nice people. I wouldn't be surprised if Glen did something to their car." Mo swallowed hard. "I know he was mad at us, but I don't understand why he'd do all this."

"Me neither."

Mo took a deep cleansing breath. "I heard the police had you locked up. Must've been scary."

Cora nodded. "I was pretty freaked, but I knew I was innocent. They never actually charged me. Who knows what would've happened if you would've ..."

"Died?"

Cora nodded again.

Mo grinned. "Lucky for you I'm indestructible."

"It does seem that way." Cora hesitated for a moment. "There's something I really wanted to ask you."

Mo showed his hands and said, "Shoot."

Cora mock-frowned.

"Too soon?"

Cora laughed.

Mo joined in. When their laughter subsided, Mo said, "What did you wanna ask?"

"In the house, when you were hurt, it was like you weren't hurt, like it didn't even bother you."

"I have congenital analgesia. It's a rare genetic disorder that causes me not to feel pain."

Cora furrowed her brow. "I've never heard of that."

"That's not surprising. It only effects about one in a million people."

"Wow. You really are one in a million. I would love not to feel pain. I cry when I stub my toe."

Mo shook his head. "It's a curse. When I was a baby, my mother had to watch me like a hawk because I would constantly hurt myself. I had no pain to train me not to do dumb shit."

"*Your burns.*"

"I had a tough time with burns. I can feel the heat, but not the burning pain."

Cora winced.

Mo held up his pinkie, missing the tip. "I bit off the tip of my finger when I was a little kid. Just after I got teeth."

Cora gasped. "Oh, my God."

"My mom kept me in mittens overnight from then on. I had to learn my limits using my brain, not my pain threshold. My mom taught me to check my body every night and every morning for swelling or redness or any sign of injury."

"I can't believe she let you play football."

"She didn't want me to. I begged and begged, and my dad let me. They almost divorced over that. They might've if …"

Cora leaned closer. "If what?"

"If she hadn't died. Brain cancer."

"I didn't know that. I'm so sorry, Mo."

Mo let out a heavy breath. "I think she was always so worried about me that she didn't take care of herself. That's on me."

Cora shook her head. "I'm sure your mother didn't think so."

Mo shrugged. "I should've listened to her, but I loved football. I told her that I was so fast that nobody would ever hurt me." Mo glanced up at ESPN, swallowed hard, then looked back at Cora. "I was wrong. Brian hit me in the knee, tore my ACL. Then at Penn State, I tore it again, but I didn't know it. I had a little swelling, but I kept playing. I was starting as a freshman, and I didn't want to lose my spot. Then, I got hit against Ohio State and lost my PCL and MCL. The trainer could move my lower leg in a 360-degree circle."

Cora felt sick to her stomach.

Mo stared at the book Cora had brought him. "The doctor told me that I'd never play football again. He said I should never even run again, that I should take up biking to keep the strain off my knee. Penn State would've kept me on scholarship, but ... I was stupid."

Cora carefully took one of his bandaged hands in hers. "You weren't. That was on Troy."

Mo shrugged again and looked at Cora. "That's water under the bridge now."

"Did Glen know about your condition?" Cora asked.

"I've never told anyone except my coaches. My mom didn't want my friends to know. She thought they would do something stupid to me, like stick me with a fork for fun or give me homemade tattoos." He hesitated. "My mom always worried that my condition would kill me, but it actually saved my life."

"Mine too. What you did was unbelievably ... brave."

Mo squeezed her hand and gazed into her eyes. "We saved each other."

Cora smiled and replied, "You're right."

Mo smiled back. "I never got to ask you about my briefcase."

Cora retracted her hand and stood from the chair, checking the open door, making sure they were alone. She sat back down and said in a low voice, "I took an Uber by the mansion yesterday, just to see if any cops were there."

Mo leaned toward Cora. "And?"

"One cop car and a crime scene investigation van."

"Maybe they'll be done by the time I get out of here."

"Then we can go together."

# Chapter 23: Cora and The Cash

Cora and Mo stepped from the car into the sun. The Uber driver turned around his Toyota Corolla and drove away. Cora and Mo walked along the country road, in the shade of oaks and maples. It had been one month since Mo had been stabbed and shot. He walked with a slight limp, using a cane for extra support, trying to keep the pressure off his injured thigh. After a short distance, they stopped at a stone bridge, a running creek below.

Instead of walking over the bridge, they walked down to the creek bed, stepping on smooth stones as they approached the water. They followed the creek, Cora leading the way, back toward the house of horrors.

Mo said, "You think it'll be there?"

Cora pivoted to Mo and waited for him to catch up. "I keep having this dream that we come down here to get the money, and the cops jump out from behind the trees and bust us."

Mo laughed, moving carefully with his cane on the uneven rocks. "That only happens in the movies. We do need to be careful about how we spend it though. And definitely do not deposit it in a bank. This is mattress money."

"Mattress money?"

Mo caught up to Cora. "My mom used to waitress at this diner. That's what she called her tips. Mattress money. She always said, 'I gotta hide this from greedy Uncle Sam.'"

Cora laughed. "This is definitely mattress money then."

They continued along the creek bed. As they neared the probable spot, Mo scoured the bank for his briefcase, but Cora looked for that downed tree.

A few minutes later, she jumped up and down, motioning toward a downed tree. "There's the tree I was telling you about."

Cora rushed to the tree, Mo limping after her. They looked along the steep embankment, behind the tree.

"I don't see it," Mo said.

"Neither do I," Cora said, her excitement fading.

They climbed over the downed tree, examining the embankment.

Cora spotted a right angle among the round creek stones. "There it is!" She ran to the briefcase, slipping and falling on the rocks, but she caught herself with her hands.

"You okay?" Mo asked, following in her direction.

She stood and smiled. "I'm fine." Then, she pointed out the edge of the briefcase, hiding behind a cluster of stones.

He smiled. "I see it."

They walked over to the briefcase, Cora moving slowly so Mo could keep pace. He picked up his briefcase and set it on a large stone, along with his cane.

Cora scanned the creek and the forest, making sure they were alone.

Mo flipped open the latches and looked at Cora, his eyebrows raised. "You didn't lock it?"

Cora frowned. "I didn't even think about locking it. I was under a bit of pressure."

He opened the briefcase and inside were tightly bound stacks of one-hundred-dollar bills. Mo chuckled and shook his head. "I can't believe it."

Cora scanned the creek and forest again.

Mo pivoted to Cora. "What's wrong? Aren't you happy?"

"I was looking for the cops."

Mo laughed, but still checked the creek and surrounding forest for signs of law enforcement. "It's just you and me."

Cora stepped dangerously close to Mo. "It is."

"You wanna have dinner with me tonight? We should celebrate."

Cora kissed him on the lips, her mouth parted just enough to rule out a friendly peck. Mo hesitated, then reciprocated. She felt his smile through his kiss. Until the mansion and Glen, she'd never fought for anything. She'd never gone after what she really wanted. *Those days are over.*

# If you enjoyed this novel, …
## you'll love *Cesspool.*

**Would you become a criminal to do the right thing?**

Disgraced teacher James Fisher moved to a backwoods town, content to live his life in solitude. He was awakened from his apathy by a small girl with a big problem. James suspected Brittany was being abused and exploited by his neighbor. He called the police but soon realized his mistake, as the neighbor was related to the chief of police.

Most would've looked the other way. Getting involved placed James squarely in the crosshairs of the local police. James lacked the brawn or the connections to save himself, much less Brittany. The police held all the power, and they knew it. But that was also their weakness. They underestimated what the mild-mannered teacher and the young runaway would do for justice.

**Buy *Cesspool* today if you enjoy vigilante justice page-turners with a side of underdog.**

Adult language and content.

Visit https://philwbooks.com/books/ to learn more.

<u>What Readers Are Saying</u>

"Wow. Just wow. This book was amazing. Every chapter, every page had me thinking about ideas, philosophies, current events, history in a different way." - Elaine ★★★★★

"The writing is excellent, the pace quick, the characters and dialog believable. An excellent read." - Dusty Sharp, Author of the Austin Conrad Series ★★★★★

"I have enjoyed this author before, but this is his best yet. If you want a story that will keep you reading, this is it. The story, the characters, and the cunning displayed by the hero is some of the best fiction I've had the pleasure to read. Do yourself a favor and pick up this book. You won't lay it down until the end." - Patrick R. ★★★★★

"Wow! This was one of the best books I've read in a while. Twists, turns, and unexpected events in every chapter. What a movie this would make." –Kindle Customer ★★★★★

"This book was incredible! I read it in three days—the entire story is a whirlwind of fantastic characters, a perfect constancy of ups and downs throughout." - Rae L. ★★★★★

# For the Reader

Dear Reader,

I'm thrilled that you took precious time out of your life to read my novel. Thank you! I hope you found it entertaining, engaging, and thought-provoking. If so, please consider writing a positive review on Amazon and Goodreads. Five-star reviews have a huge impact on future sales. The review doesn't need to be long and detailed, if you're more of a reader than a writer. As an author and a small businessman, competing against the big publishers, I greatly appreciate every reader, every review, and every referral.

**If you're interested in receiving my novel *Against the Grain* for free and/or reading my other titles for free or discounted, go to the following link:** http://www.PhilWBooks.com. You're probably thinking, *What's the catch?* There is no catch.

If you want to contact me, don't be bashful. I can be found at Phil@PhilWBooks.com. I do my best to respond to all emails.

Sincerely,
Phil M. Williams

# Gratitude

I'd like to thank my wife for being my first reader, sounding board, and cheerleader. Without her support and unwavering belief in my skill as an author, I'm not sure I would have embarked on this career. I love you, Denise.

I'd also like to thank my editors. My developmental editor, Caroline Smailes, did a fantastic job finding the holes in my plot and suggesting remedies. As always, my line editor, Denise Barker (not to be confused with my wife, Denise Williams), did a fantastic job making sure the manuscript was error-free. I love her comments and feedback.

Thank you to my beta readers, Sue, Saundra, Ray, and Ann. They're my last defense against the dreaded typo. Thank you to my mother-in-law, Joy. As a retired nurse, she is a wealth of knowledge for all things medical, and always gracious with her time. Many of our conversations start with, "So, I shot this guy …"

And finally, thank you to you, the reader. Without you I wouldn't have a career. As long as you keep reading, I'll keep writing.

www.ingramcontent.com/pod-product-compliance
Lightning Source LLC
Chambersburg PA
CBHW022036170626
46808CB00003B/1225